S0-ART-644

Ride a Paper Tiger

WILLIAM ASH

Ride a Paper Tiger

Walker and Company
New York

First published in the United States of America in 1969 by Walker and Company, a division of the Walker Publishing Company, Inc.

Library of Congress Catalog Card Number: 69-15712.

Printed in the United States of America from type set in Great Britain.

Contents

1	On the Run	7
2	He Makes Us Laugh	24
3	It's Nice to be Trusted	41
4	I May be Falling in Love	55
5	Just for the Ride	71
6	We Believe You Can Swing It	88
7	Madrugada Roja	104
8	A Favourable Exchange?	119
9	You Can Stop Talking. You're Dead	135
10	It's Not Your Country	151
11	An Ordinary Kitchen Knife	166
12	A Red Carpet of Ponchos	181

I

'On the Run'

A FEW tourists who make a really determined effort to avoid their kind by getting well off the beaten track fetch up at the Hotel *Buena Vista* in San Pedro. There they have the doubtful consolation of knowing that any gringo they meet has failed just as miserably in eluding his fellows as they have themselves. This attitude has the effect of making anyone from north of the Rio Grande look at once furtive and ill-tempered—like a small-time crook who has just been cheated. That is the impression I must have given as I entered the grand salon which stretches along one side of the building and through adobe arches provides a magnificent view of the Cordilleras.

I was determined to avoid a fat American I had glimpsed earlier so that I could feel sorry for myself in my enforced exile without interruption. I sat at a little table precariously balanced on the uneven brick floor, tall iced drink before me, with every intention of putting in several hours' intensive sulking before dinner.

The great empty plain darkened with shadows and the high jagged peaks glowed orange in the setting sun. Such natural extravagance made it difficult to give myself up as completely as I would have liked to a mood of self-com-miseration. I somewhat pointedly moved my chair and turned my back on the mountains. As I did so, I noticed the fat man who had just come into the room from the patio and was looking for a place to sit.

The only chair unoccupied by the better-off locals who

patronised the hotel was at my table; but I certainly did not encourage him to join me. He respected my glower to the extent of once more glancing around the room to see if there was another vacancy and then, with a shrug, crossed over to put his hand on the back of the chair opposite me.

'May I?'

I shrugged in acquiescence and he sat down heavily, the chair teetering noisily on the rough floor.

'Ride it, cowboy,' I muttered to myself.

He dabbed at his damp forehead with a large handkerchief and, when the waiter came to the table to take his order, he pointed at my drink. 'I'll have one of those.'

'Sí, señor—a daiquiri.'

I waited for it as one awaits any act of trivial inevitability like a dropped second shoe or a heralded sneeze and finally he said : 'Been a hot day.'

I could have told him that hot dry days were to be expected at this latitude and, like the coolness of the nights at such an altitude, was one of the reasons people came at all to this part of Central America. But all I actually said was, 'Yes.'

His small eyes moved around the room and gazed out past me to the burnished slopes. 'Picturesque, though,' he granted.

'Look,' I remonstrated with a tested patience. 'I realise that it's difficult to maintain a thoroughly petty churlishness amid scenes of such natural grandeur; but I think we ought to try.'

'Sorry,' he said with a hurt look.

'Nothing personal, you understand.'

'Of course.' But his heavy body had crumpled a bit at this unexpected rebuff, rocking his chair forward and upsetting the balance of the table so that my drink was spilt. 'Sorry,' he said again and held out his handkerchief.

8

I waived the offer and dabbed at my trousers with a paper napkin. Was he really the sort of clumsy but amiable nuisance it is impossible to dislike, I asked myself—or was he exploiting the probability of my taking him as such to cover a determined assault on my privacy? I spent a few moments turning over these alternative readings of his character till I realised that, objectively speaking, the results in terms of my wish to keep to myself would be precisely the same in either case.

All my life I have made the mistake of paralysing myself with endless surmises about the motives of those around me while they, quite cheerfully and ruthlessly, went on doing things to me which kept altering the relationship I was trying to analyse. Why, just for a change, should I not do things to others and let *them* worry about what had prompted such actions? I glanced up at that fat, slightly obsequious face with the thought that I should have spilt a drink on *him,* at the very beginning.

'Maybe I ought to introduce myself,' he said.

'Not necessarily,' I demurred. 'Unless you feel that it adds something to an acquaintanceship which never gets started to know the name of the person you've successfully avoided.'

He laughed—more a self-conscious giggle really. 'You've got a point there,' just as if I were subtly encouraging an exchange of names instead of tactfully repudiating it. 'I'm Horace Watson.'

'Nice not to've got to know you, Mr. Watson. And the person you didn't quite hit it off with that day in the Hotel *Buena Vista* is Kyle Brandeis.'

'You on vacation?'

I shook my head. 'On the run.'

'Oh,' he said.

I leaned back resignedly. 'Well?' perfectly aware of the

9

fact that he was going to tell me what he was doing there whether I asked him to or not.

'I'm on a business trip.' He handed me a card.

'Representative of Allied Chemicals Inc.,' I read. 'Medical supplies, including the wonder drug—Metazone.'

'You can keep it,' he said. 'The idea was that I'd work some of the areas where the latest medicines haven't penetrated yet.'

'Yes. Well at the moment I feel fine—physically, that is. But if I seem to have a headache coming on or . . .'

'We only distribute on a wholesale basis, of course. But I've got plenty of samples with me, so if you *should* be feeling a little under the weather . . .'

'Very kind; but the climate suits me.'

The waiter brought a tray with my table companion's drink and a folded note for me.

I opened it and read: 'Are you the Brandeis who teaches at Columbia?' It was signed simply 'G'.

I looked up enquiringly at the waiter and he indicated a well-dressed man who was standing at the bar, a little apart from the others drinking there. He met my glance and smiled in acknowledgement of the note I held.

'Will you excuse me?' I asked Watson, delighted to be able to make my escape from him. 'Someone wishes to speak with me.'

'Sure. Sorry to've butted in on you like that, but . . .' As he tilted back in his chair, his knees hit the table and sloshed his own daiquiri over his trousers.

'Don't mention it.' I handed him a paper napkin and walked across to the bar.

'Ah, Mr. Brandeis,' the writer of the note held out his hand cordially. 'My name is Gabaldon, Rafael Gabaldon. May I order something for you? Perhaps we could go into the patio. It's too crowded here to talk.'

I assented and when the barman had mixed me another drink I followed him through the open glass door to a bench beneath a flowering shrub which had stained the pavement crimson with fallen petals. It was already cooler and a vagrant breeze ruffled the water in the basin of the non-functioning fountain.

'I am expecting a guest from the capital,' Gabaldon explained. 'I saw your name while I was looking through the register. I wondered if it could be the Brandeis whose literary criticism I had read in the pages of the *Western Review*.'

I looked at him curiously. The face, still handsome for all his fifty or so years, was completely grave and polite.

'You look sceptical,' he said with a gracious smile.

'As editor of the *Review* and, for financial reasons, chief contributor, I never achieved so much fame that being recognised in an out-of-the-way corner of Central America should not cause me some surprise—even,' I added, 'if such recognition comes from one as widely-read in the literature of the North as your impeccable English proclaims you, señor.'

He bowed slightly.

'Frankly,' I continued, 'I suspected a leg-pull.'

'You're too modest, Mr. Brandeis—though I confess that it was in connection with a particular article that your name became known to me.'

'Yes?'

'Your appreciation of the work of one of our greatest, if not *the* greatest, living poet.'

'Of course. Manuel Ortiz. I did that piece—let's see, it must be several years ago now. When the first volume of translations came out in the States.'

'Manuel Ortiz is a good friend of mine. I almost said *was* a good friend of mine. It's difficult not to think in the past tense of one who has been imprisoned so long.'

11

'I understand. For a time I was associated with the "Free Ortiz Committee" which had some support on university campuses, circulating petitions and that sort of thing.'

Gabaldon shot a quick look at me. 'Has that anything to do with your present visit?'

'No. The Committee petered out some time ago. I'm here as a—well, a refugee you might say.'

'Because of your protests against injustice?'

'I wish I could say it was that. I'd rather fancy myself as a victim of political persecution. But I'm really English, though I've lived in the States for many years, and the authorities have never taken me very seriously. I didn't even have to sign a loyalty oath. No, I'm afraid it's a purely personal matter.'

'But you'll at least make some attempt to see Ortiz while you're here.'

'Frankly I hadn't thought of him till you mentioned that article of mine. I know it must sound callous; but we Anglo-Saxons have a wonderful capacity for not letting other peoples' miseries distract us from our private problems.'

'I believe you're too hard on yourself, Mr. Brandeis. Your article was a magnificent tribute to a fellow writer who has suffered for his principles. It could only have been written by a man of great compassion as well as true literary discrimination.'

'You'd be surprised how much genuine feeling I can trump up when a deadline is about to catch me with a half empty *Review* on my hands.'

Gabaldon got up. 'I think I see the man I was expecting. I'd like to talk to you some more about poor Ortiz. Would you consent to dine with me tonight?'

'Well I . . .'

'It would be a great kindness if you'd come. About nine,

shall we say? It's that white house on the right of the road leading down to the town.'

'The one with the ironwork gates?'

'That's it. My family and I shall be honoured to share our informal meal with you.'

'Well, thanks.'

'Till nine, then, Mr. Brandeis.' He saluted me courteously and returned to the salon.

I went up to my room to lie down for a while before having a shower and dressing.

When I came down to the lounge several hours later, my fat acquaintance, Watson, was standing near the front door smoking a large cigar. He waved his hand and grinned broadly—just as if the efforts I had made not to get to know him constituted a very special bond between us.

'Who was that distinguished-looking fellow you were talking to?' he asked.

'A certain Señor Gabaldon,' I answered shortly. 'I don't think he runs a drug store.'

'Of course not,' Watson laughed. 'I was just curious. He looks so much like a Spanish nobleman.'

'Curious as to how *I* would have access to such circles?' I asked.

'I guess so. You know,' screwing his face up shrewdly and pointing at me with the fingers holding the enormous cigar, 'I kind of figured there was more to you than meets the eye.'

'It's the impression I always try to give,' I told him, brushing the ash of his cigar from my coat sleeve.

'Sorry,' he apologised and made a few clumsy swipes himself at my sleeve.

'Don't mention it. Keeps out moths they say.'

I walked past him toward the door and he called after me with an execrable accent, 'Hasta mañana.' I was be-

ginning to wonder if he was quite so harmless as he
seemed. Certainly, if the relationship continued in spite
of anything I could do about it, we looked like finishing
off my scanty wardrobe at an alarming rate.

I went down the stairs and took the road which curved
away from the hotel. Below me were the lights of San
Pedro, then the dark jagged band of the peaks and, above,
the bright stars. There was a fragrance in the clear air—
some exotic, night-flowering plant; and I breathed deeply
as I strode the short distance down the slope to the massive gates of the Gabaldon residence.

A gravel drive led to the house—a large, white-washed
structure which seemed to glow luminously against the
star-punctured back-drop of the sky. I climbed the steps
and banged the brass knocker. The heavy, studded door
was opened by a very lovely young woman in her early
twenties.

'You must be Mr. Brandeis,' she said with a charming
smile.

'For once,' I told her gallantly, 'it's a pleasure to admit
it.'

'My father is arranging a business matter with a col-
league who arrived today from the capital. He asked me to
express his regret at not having finished before you came.
But he won't be long.'

'I hope he won't rush things for my sake.'

I followed her across the hall and into a large sitting
room at the back of the house.

'Would you like a drink, Mr. Brandeis?'

'Not particularly.' I strolled over to the windows and
stood looking out beyond a paved terrace to the lights of
town.

'I didn't think you people ever refused a drink,' she said
with light-hearted malice.

'It's one of the forms a mild tendency toward subversion occasionally takes with me.'

'Would you like to go out on the terrace?'

She opened a door which led into a small courtyard covered by a projection of the tile roof, and we stepped out onto the pavement which ran the length of the house. I pointed to the large ornamental urns at either end. 'That's too much, I think. I was prepared to accept your father's old-world courtesy, this magnificent house, even you, Señorita Gabaldon; but those two perfectly-sited urns are just that last touch too much which convinces me it's all unreal. And now that I've seen through the imposture, perhaps you'll take off that lovely mask and we can carry on at a more ordinary level where I won't feel at such a disadvantage.'

'You're very kind, Mr. Brandeis; but I assure you that it's we who are honoured by the visit of such a distinguished author.'

'I don't know about that,' I said wryly. 'If critics are unsuccessful novelists, then I suspect that editors of small literary reviews are unsuccessful critics.' I looked down the slope which was covered with trees set out in order and filling all the space between the house and the first lights of the town. 'What're those?'

'Orange trees.'

'Do they work?'

'Yes, indeed. There're several artesian wells which provide water for irrigation.'

'And that's the material basis for all this?' with a gesture taking in the house and herself and not leaving out the urns.

'There's cattle also, on the uplands beyond San Pedro.'

'And all that land belongs to your father?'

'No, not for many years. It was broken up at one time and then, seven or eight years ago, it was all reincorporated as a venture subsidised by business men in the capital. That's what my father's discussing now. He's really just a manager paid by the firm. Even this house doesn't actually belong to us any more.'

'There's one thing that puzzles me. How did a man like your father come to be the friend of a revolutionary poet behind bars?'

'They knew each other at the University. As you know, Manuel Ortiz comes from a very different background. His father was a stone mason who was killed during the disturbances in 'fourteen—when Manuel was just a baby. His mother worked herself to death helping him to get a good education. But that difference in origin didn't prevent Ortiz and my father from becoming close friends.'

'But surely your father doesn't share the views which got Ortiz locked up.'

'No. Father's at most an old-fashioned liberal. But political differences didn't seem to disrupt their friendship either. I remember Tio Manuel staying with us often when I was a child. I was fascinated by his hands—broad peon's hands, with strong stubby fingers. You could hardly imagine a pen in such hands. He used to make up funny verses for Juanito and me.'

I watched her lovely eyes fixed on that past time, the reminiscent smile which played on her lips.

'Such a wonderful man,' she went on, eyes glistening, 'with such a heart—a heart big enough to hold all the woes of this unhappy country.' Then, with a little shake of her head, eyes flashing now: 'And those pigs shut him up. As if you could ever silence that tongue! How can prison walls divide a man like that from the people who love him?'

She seemed to expect some response from me. 'What did you say?' I could only ask, so rapt in how she looked that I had not been following her words very closely.

16

'How can he be left there year after year?' She turned those lovely eyes full on me in earnest entreaty. 'Perhaps you've come with some idea of what we can do to get him released.'

'Well,' rubbing my forehead, reflectively, 'that's something I've been wanting to clear up. People seem to be jumping to the conclusion that my coming to Central America is somehow connected with the interest—mainly literary, mind you—I once expressed in Manuel Ortiz. That's not true. And it's merely a coincidence that with my past concern for the poet's work I've landed amongst those for whom his present incarceration is still a very live matter.'

'Why *did* you come here, Mr. Brandeis?'

'I don't really think I . . .'

'If you're engaged in some *confidential* scheme on behalf of Tio Manuel, then of course I shouldn't have . . .'

'No, wait a minute, Señorita Gabaldon. It isn't that at all. My reluctance to speak of my reasons for skipping across the border is simply that I'm not very proud of them. I'd better explain the whole thing to avoid any further confusion. I've a couple of very good reasons for taking it on the lam—these two wives of mine.'

'You're a bigamist!' she exclaimed.

'They didn't run concurrently. I was divorced from my first wife so that I could marry my second. I was divorced from my second because I'd discovered, a little late in the day I admit, that I'm not the marrying kind. Anyway, what with rising costs of bringing out my *Review* and an unexpanding readership, I couldn't keep up my alimony payments. This is all rather sordid,' I broke off. 'If you think my life story is unsuited to the ears of a young woman like yourself . . .'

'Go ahead,' she urged. 'I don't believe in being sheltered from the less seemly aspects of life.'

17

'I see. Well, not to bore you with more details of my squalid past, I decided to light out for a while. I can collect material for the *Review* wherever I happen to be; I write most of it myself anyway; and I have an arrangement with the printers to go on bringing out the periodical month by month. Meanwhile it'll take my wives' lawyers some time to catch up with me—long enough, perhaps, for me to get my head above water again. That's why I chose an out-of-the-way place like San Pedro.'

'Leaving those two poor women you've deserted to starve!'

'Poor women, my foot! They're both able-bodied Amazons perfectly capable of supporting themselves. Do them good to stop lying on their backs at my expense. In fact, they might even marry the men they've taken up with, once they find they're not getting any more out of me for a bit.'

'Is refusing to pay alimony an extraditable offence?'

'I don't know. Uncle Sam and the boys who've got your Tio Manuel in jug will have to work it out between them—once they've run me to earth. The fact that I'm English may be an added complication; but I don't know for whom.'

She considered me with an interest I found rather ambiguous. 'You must be very attractive to women, Mr. Brandeis.'

'Because I'm so spineless, you mean.'

We turned at the sound of footsteps on the pavement. Señor Gabaldon came forward with his hand outstretched for a welcoming clasp.

'Please forgive me for proving such a poor host. Ana, you haven't even given our guest a drink.'

'Short of putting a hammer lock on me and forcing one

down my throat, she couldn't have done more,' I assured him.

'Come,' he linked his arm in mine and led me back into the house. 'We'll have supper while we talk.'

In the dining room on a large table there were dishes of cold salad, a savoury meat mixture and steaming tortillas—in fact, all the raw materials for fabricating our own tacos. Presiding over the spread was Gabaldon's charming wife to whom he presented me.

'You've met all my family now, except for my son, Juan. But,' with a slight thinning of his mouth, 'we see very little of Juan these days ourselves.'

'You'll make Mr. Brandeis think my brother's up to some mischief,' Ana protested.

'Isn't he?'

'Not mischief, papa.'

'We won't speak of it now.'

'You always get these problems between different generations.' I said as I heaped a plate from the various dishes. '*My* father insisted that *I'd* come to a bad end, and I couldn't bear to disappoint him. But I never got any credit for such filial consideration.'

'Since we met this afternoon,' Señor Gabaldon told me, 'I've been thinking how it might be possible for you to see Ortiz.'

'Yes,' doubtfully.

'I believe the best plan is for you to be quite open about it. Let the press in the capital know that you represent those in the States who admire Manuel's work, that you insist on the right to interview him on the subject of contemporary poetry for your journal. After all, I don't believe the authorities would wish to alienate a well-known literary editor from the north if they could help it. You should also let your own embassy know that you wish to see him—as a poet, not as a political prisoner. I'm sure they could bring pressure to bear.'

'But *would* they?' I countered. 'I mean, let's not kid ourselves that the government of my adopted country is firmly opposed to locking up reds just because they haven't done anything illegal.'

'True enough, Mr. Brandeis. But that government and mine like to give a liberal gloss to their actions if it doesn't cost too much. It might be felt that allowing you to see Ortiz, possibly to report that he isn't being treated too badly . . .'

'If he isn't!' Ana interjected sarcastically.

'It might be felt that such an interview would allay some of the criticism about keeping so great a man in prison.'

'Ah, but do we *want* to allay that criticism, Señor Gabaldon? Wouldn't we be playing into their hands?'

'The fact that your interview would be *thought* to have that effect, doesn't mean that it actually would. The effect is really going to depend on how you write up the interview afterwards, isn't it? Surely a writer of your skill could accede formally to the limitations *they* impose and yet bring off the results *we* intend.'

'Oh well, if you appeal to my vanity . . . But there's still one major difficulty,' I said, carefully avoiding Ana's eyes. 'I'm most anxious on this trip not to court any publicity.'

'Sometimes,' with a faint frown, 'your modesty seems almost excessive, Mr. Brandeis.'

'But fully justified, Señor Gabaldon, I assure you.'

'Please help yourself to something more,' the Señora encouraged.

'Thank you. I *will* have just another nibble of salad; and a spot of this delicious meat preparation, of course; and perhaps just one more tortilla, or maybe two.'

'Your appetite does my mother's food great credit,' Ana said. 'You obviously miss home cooking.'

'But in my experience home cooking was never like this. Had it been, believe me my whole life might've taken a different course.'

I finished eating long after every one else; and the three of us went into the sitting room while Señora Gabaldon made coffee.

I accepted a glass of brandy and a cigar. After such hospitality, I could hardly not say : 'I'll think about what you've suggested. Something along those lines may well be possible.'

'Naturally,' Señor Gabaldon said, 'my family and I have a strong personal interest in this matter. We would be so grateful for a chance, through you, of conveying our warmest greetings to our old friend.'

'Do you write to him?'

'We do; but we've no way of knowing if he receives our letters. Certainly we hear nothing in reply.'

'How long has Ortiz been in prison now?'

'Over six years.'

'It's terrible. Do you suppose he still holds, quite unchanged, the views which led to his imprisonment?'

'I'm sure of it. They'd have let him out otherwise. A recantation by their most famous opponent would be quite a feather in their cap.'

'Tio Manuel will never change,' Ana said proudly— 'not if they threatened to kill him.'

'As they did at first,' he remarked. 'It was only a flood of protests which forced them to commute his sentence to life imprisonment.'

'Tell me, Señor Gabaldon,' I challenged him, 'would you like to see the sort of country Manuel Ortiz would bring into being if he could?'

He paused only a moment before answering with a

shrug: 'If it's the country the people want, I'd have to accept it, wouldn't I?'

Coffee was brought in and we talked generally for a while about points of interest I might see during my stay at San Pedro.

'There're some ancient Indian ruins about ten miles from here. Nothing very impressive, I suppose, but typical.'

'Might have a look. How does one get there?'

'You can take a local bus, or hire a car. The best way is to ride up over the Silla Pass. Ana could guide you there if you'd like to borrow one of our horses.'

'Providing Mr. Brandeis *can* ride.'

'If you've got a horse that thinks it can stay under me. Some can't manage it. I'm too tricky for them.'

I looked at my watch. 'I think I should be getting back to the hotel. Thank you for such a pleasant evening.'

'We'll talk again about your trying to see Ortiz.'

'Of course. Goodnight, Señora.'

Ana accompanied me to the door. 'Don't let my father bully you into seeing our insignificant ruins, if you don't want to.'

'Don't let him bully you into taking me there, if *you* don't want to.'

'You might've spared my maidenly reticence by letting me do it as a dutiful daughter.'

'Nope. Cards face up on the table. That's the way I like to play. It's probably why I always lose.'

'That's not the way I heard it, Mr. Brandeis.'

'If you call what's happened to me *winning,* I think I'll cash in my chips. Goodnight, Señorita Gabaldon.'

'Goodnight.'

I walked up the road humming softly. 'Nice people,' I broke off at one point to say to myself. And I added: 'You're not used to dealing with nice people, Kyle boy. If you're smart, you'll sneak out of San Pedro as quickly as possible.' It cost nothing to tell myself that, because I knew I was not smart.

Just before I got back to the hotel I became aware that someone was following me. I was so certain of this that instead of going up the steps I turned off the path and stood behind a eucalyptus tree.

There *was* someone—a slender young man who walked beyond the point where I had left the path and then paused. He stood there looking around. For me? I wondered. I was about to step forth and ask him what he wanted when there was a heavy tread on the stairs and Watson came into view. He glanced behind him and, apparently assuring himself that he was not being watched, crossed over to the young man. They talked together too quietly for me to hear what they were saying.

I shrugged and tiptoed away to enter the hotel by a side door. 'It's a funny way to sell drugs,' I muttered.

2

'He Makes Us Laugh'

I WOKE up late the next morning, which was a Sunday, and dressed to the sound of church bells throbbing in the town below. Downstairs in the restaurant I had a cup of coffee and some toast, in the thick of a party of tourists who must have arrived during the night.

I decided that I could give them the slip by walking into town when most of them would be going down by car and found myself on the dusty road with a couple of dozen Americans who must have had the same idea about me. No wonder 'Yanks Go Home' had taken the place of amorous scratchings on walls all over the world. With a bucket of paint and a brush I could cheerfully have added to such graffiti—while admitting, of course, that I might be motivated by envy of those who had supplanted my own countrymen as objects of universal dislike.

I mooched along gloomily with these unsought companions, visiting the central market where most of the stalls were open for business in spite of its being a holy day. I stood by, secretly willing the locals to fleece the visitors soundly over every transaction in order to shorten the length of their stay. I drifted along with them to the main plaza where we stood for a while gaping up at the ornate stone work of the baroque cathedral; and then, still with this company I had been thrown with for some atrocious crime committed in a previous life, plodded into a restaurant for lunch.

It was a very hot day and most of the overblown wives

fanning themselves at the tables and even their less obese mates who had divested themselves of jackets and opened their collars were all visibly suffering. Heat, I realised, was my only ally in any attempt to shake them.

On the walls of the little restaurant were colourful posters advertising a bull fight that afternoon in the amphitheatre on the outskirts of town. If I bought one of the cheaper tickets on the sunny side . . .

I tried to remember whether I had any scruples against bull fighting as such. This consisted of reviewing the various causes and movements I had at different times been vaguely associated with to recall if I had ever actually signed any petition or subscribed any resolution specifically directed against the public immolation of bulls. I finally settled the matter to my own satisfaction on the principle that when we had a world from which injustice to men had been abolished, it would be time enough to take up the question of a fair deal for animals.

My ruse was largely successful. About three o'clock in the afternoon I was sitting on a hard seat in the full blaze of the sun with hardly a gringo in sight. The exception was Horace Watson whose fat bulk was planted four or five rows in front of me. This did not bother me very much. In between the dispatch of the bulls I could watch him melt away like butter in a frying pan.

He was sitting beside the slender young man I had seen him in conversation with last night. 'Ah well,' with a certain liberal indifference, 'there's no accounting for human tastes'—referring more to the handsome youth than to any sexual aberration on Watson's part. He glanced up and seemed a bit discomfited by my presence; but after a moment's hesitation he waved.

I ignored the gesture on the ground that when I am wearing dark glasses others ought to respect my feeling that I am quite unrecognisable.

Some while later a man with a pock-marked face took the seat beside me. He was addressed as Pérez by the friend who accompanied him; and when Pérez discovered that I had some smattering of Spanish, he took it upon himself to tell me something about the principals in that day's programme.

'These,' he pointed to the first two names on the crumpled list he held for my inspection—'old women! And Baroja,' he tapped his head—'he's crazy, that one. He makes up his mind how he's going to fight before he even sees the bull, I think. If it happens to suit the bull he draws, then we may see something. Otherwise,' he shrugged elaborately, 'we'll be watching a clown.'

'I see,' I said with every show of intelligent interest.

'But then,' Pérez informed me, 'you wouldn't expect to get the best toreros in a little town like this. Only once or twice a year on feast days. We have to be content with spotting the young ones who may *become* great. Like this one,' indicating another name on the list—'Nuñez. You watch him, señor. He looks clumsy, but that is only a trick to deceive.'

'To deceive us or the bull?'

'I had not thought of that.' Pérez scratched his head. 'It looks dangerous because he works the bull very close and he does not seem to know what he is doing and the crowd gets excited; but the bull . . .'

'The bull sees through the whole thing I suppose.'

That made Pérez laugh loudly. He turned and repeated my remark to his companion who also laughed loudly and told the man beyond. In this way laughter ran right down to the end of the row where the last man laughed too and asked a question of the one who had told him what I said. Eventually the question got back to me.

'My friends want to know why you sit on the sunny side,' Pérez asked.

'To get away from *my* friends,' I explained.

This information was relayed back and somewhere along the line I heard the word 'Castro' mentioned.

'Sí,' I took it up at once. 'Viva Castro!'

Pérez clapped me on the back in high good humour. 'Viva Castro!' he said; and others in our row called out laughingly, 'Viva Castro!' till certain people in the crowd began to regard us with some annoyance.

The hot still afternoon was suddenly shattered by the blast of trumpets. The local band, making up in individual enthusiasm what it lacked in togetherness, played a spirited march; and a ragged parade of those who were to perform, several astride very weary looking horses, came into the arena. They made one complete circuit, stopping from time to time to bow to the spectators, and then withdrew.

A gate was raised and a smallish but very fierce black bull rushed into the middle of the ring, tried to toss the darts off its back and then loped around the arena just inside the barriers.

I had assumed that my sympathies would be with the bull; but the humans I had seen in their tawdry, much-repaired uniforms looked so pathetic that I could not see how the whole lot of them would ever manage to cope with that animal fury charging around the ring. This impression was strengthened by the long time the arena seemed to be left to the bull before a man came out with a cape, made a few highly tentative passes and scuttled behind one of the barriers.

'Hooks low and to the left,' Pérez confided.

'Doesn't he, though,' I nodded knowingly.

Picador and banderillero did their work and eventually, just below us, there was a rather messy kill which brought jeers from the crowd.

While the bull was being dragged across the sand, I

hailed a boy lugging bottled drinks up the aisle and bought luke-warm beer for my amigos along the row. They held up their bottles toward me before imbibing. 'Salud!' And I pledged them in turn.

I was enjoying myself thoroughly; and then Pérez did a very strange thing. He stood up and emptied his bottle over a group of tough-looking chaps sitting two rows in front of us. Having done so, he thrust the bottle toward me and like a goop I took it. When angry faces turned in our direction, there was I with a silly expression on my face, holding a bottle in each hand, while Pérez regarded me with a look all innocent surprise.

Several of the men who had been splashed with the beer were coming up the aisle. Others were pushing their way past spectators, climbing over the seats to get at me.

'Viva Castro!' I quavered hopefully. It had no effect at all on those enraged men shouting at me volubly as they advanced.

I glanced aside and saw that Pérez and his friend had disappeared. I decided that I had better do the same and I backed rapidly up the aisle with a half-dozen infuriated men in hot pursuit. I tried to explain what had happened; but my Spanish was not equal to such an occasion and they were making so much noise I doubt if they would have heard me anyway.

Suddenly my sympathies were all with the bull again. I could see myself being finished off just as messily right there in the stands.

Someone plucked at my sleeve. I turned and saw Pérez. 'This way, señor—quickly.'

He dashed down the stairs of one of the exits and ran along the circular corridor inside the building with me panting close behind him. I could still hear those who were chasing me and this enabled me to keep up with

Pérez in spite of a profound disinclination for such energetic activity on so hot a day.

We ran half way around the building and plunged down a flight of stairs and out into the blinding sunlight. There, waiting for us, was an ancient Ford with Pérez' friend behind the wheel.

'Inside, señor.'

I climbed in and after several loud backfires we drove off in a cloud of smoke, like something in an old Keystone comedy.

When I got my breath back, I asked Pérez what in the hell this was all about. He merely put his finger on his lips to indicate that he had no intention of telling me.

We bumped a short distance along unpaved streets in the poorer section of town and pulled up in front of an adobe hut set somewhat apart from similar dwellings in the same road.

Pérez got out of the car and held back the worn curtain which screened the doorway. 'Welcome, señor, to my humble abode.'

'What is this?' I asked again.

'It's cooler inside,' was his only answer.

His friend nudged me gently from behind and, frowning deeply, I entered the cool dark interior smelling strongly of onions.

As soon as we were inside, Pérez and his friend collapsed into each other's arms laughing till the tears streamed down their faces.

'Go on!' I said shortly. 'It wasn't that funny. If those guys had beaten me half to death, *that* might've been worth a few chuckles.'

'They wouldn't hurt anybody. They just wanted to argue about it. If you pour beer over people, it's only fair, señor, to let them have their say.'

'But *I* didn't pour beer over them. *You* did. I know it

wasn't very good beer; but all the same . . .'

'Well,' scratching his head, 'we were told to get you to come here. That's what we were told to do. But how we were to do it—Ah,' with a smile, 'that was our own idea.'

'Ingenious. But why didn't you just ask me to come?'

'No good,' Pérez shook his head. 'Would a North American gentleman come willingly to a poor house like mine?'

'I suppose,' trying to see their side of it, 'you couldn't have known on such a short acquaintance that I'm not exactly an American, to say nothing of whether I'm a gentleman. But *who* told you to bring me here?'

'He will be here soon. He will explain it himself.'

'Then I'm a prisoner meanwhile?'

'Oh señor!' Pérez seemed genuinely hurt. 'You're my guest. May I get you some fruit, or something to drink?'

'A glass of water would be most welcome.'

'Rosa!' he called. And when a buxom woman appeared at the door to the back of the house: 'Some water and a plate of fruit for our guest.'

She looked at me, giggled and withdrew.

'There is one thing I'm sorry about,' Pérez said sadly. 'We left before you had the opportunity of seeing Nuñez fight.'

'Yes,' his friend agreed. 'That was a pity.'

'Some other feast day perhaps,' I said philosophically. 'And next time the drinks can be on you.'

The woman brought in a tray, glanced at me covertly and had to leave the room at once to conceal the laughter which shook her plump shoulders.

I tried not to grin myself at the innocent amusement I gave these people—just as one endeavours not to laugh at his own jokes. There seemed to be a great future opening up for me in this country as a natural comedian.

I drank several glasses of water and peeled one of the

oranges, thinking as I did so of that orchard sloping up from the town and the lovely young woman who had described it to me the night before. No doubt I would succeed in making her laugh too.

Pérez and his friend kept up a quick run of polite chatter, stopping frequently to help me catch up with them. They paused and looked toward the door.

I turned and saw the slender young man I had already noticed several times lift the curtain and come in. He shook hands with the others and stood in front of me, hands on his narrow hips, looking me up and down with an intense but not unpleasant regard.

Something about his appearance suddenly clicked with my recent reflections about the pleasant evening I had spent at that white house half way up the hill. 'Juan Gabaldon, I believe.' I held out my hand.

He smiled slightly and took it. 'How do you know who I am?'

'There's a family resemblance. I've enjoyed your father's hospitality. But then,' smiling myself, 'you know that, don't you?'

'Yes, I know that. Please sit down, Mr. Brandeis.' He turned to Pérez. 'Could Rosa make some coffee for us?'

'Sí, Juanito.' He went out of the room.

'And now,' turning back to me, 'would you explain why you've come here?'

'But thousands of us come here every year. Perhaps you haven't heard that tourism is Latin America's number one industry.'

'We've heard,' with a grimace, 'haven't we, Tomás?'

'Sí,' the man bared his teeth in a smile—'like locusts.'

'Well, there you are then,' I told him. 'The big U.S. corporations pump money out of Central America and American tourists bring a small proportion of it back here to invest in night clubs and curio shops. It's what's called a Good Neighbour policy. Naturally, I like to do my bit to support this equitable arrangement.'

'Let me put it this way, Mr. Brandeis. Why did you choose San Pedro as the scene of your contribution toward maintaining the balance of trade?'

'It's not very patriotic of you to doubt San Pedro's attractions. Why, the front of the cathedral itself is worth a side trip from the capital—to say nothing of the majestic sweep of the Cordilleras. Where's your local pride?'

'When are you going to stop fencing with me?' he asked with a lift of his eyebrows.

'When you tell me why you got Pérez and Tomás to bring me here.'

'But that's simple. So that I could ask you why you've come to San Pedro.'

'It's not quite that simple,' I objected. 'I don't believe the local chamber of commerce has appointed *you* to find out why visitors come. In fact, I can't see that you have any right at all to ask me what I'm doing here. If you had, you'd have found a less melodramatic way of arranging an interview.'

'I'm sorry about that; but under the circumstances this is the only place where we can talk.'

'Under *your* circumstances, perhaps. I can talk anywhere. Friends tell me I always do.'

Pérez brought in four glazed cups, brilliantly-coloured, and handed them to us.

'It's not the least of the country's charms,' I said in appreciation—'sensible, man-sized coffee cups.'

'You're not going to pretend,' Juan smiled, 'that you're here as an expert on our local pottery.'

'I'm not pretending anything,' I told him irritably. 'There's no mystery about why I'm here. I thought—mistakenly on all counts—that this might prove a nice quiet spot, unfrequented by tourists, where I could spend a few months unmolested. That's all there is to it. I know it must seem like an anticlimax after the efforts you've made to wring this information from me; but that's your fault, isn't it?'

Juan Gabaldon took out a packet of cigarettes and offered one to each of us. 'That's not quite all there is to it, Mr. Brandeis. You had not been here more than a day or so when your interest in Manuel Ortiz had put you in touch with my father. Last night you managed to see me in discussion with a man called Watson; and then, this afternoon, you chose to sit on the sunny side of the stands so that you could watch us when we met again. Surely you're not going to argue that those are the actions of an ordinary tourist.'

I leaned back in the cane chair with a thoughtful frown. Put like that I almost wondered myself if I might not be up to something sneaky. But one can carry the business of seeing the other person's point of view too far.

'As for meeting your father,' I told him, 'the approach was entirely from his side, as you could soon discover by asking him. In respect to Watson I can only say that I've probably tried too hard to avoid the man to succeed altogether in doing so. I think a man would have to have a very guilty conscience to put the construction you have on a few coincidences.'

The young man smiled sceptically.

'Look,' I continued. 'A chance remark of your father's suggested to me last night that you may be involved in something of which he disapproves. Watson may be your accomplice for all I know. I assure you that I'm blissfully unaware of what it's all about; and I want to stay that way. I'm willing to forget this whole episode and, considering everything, I think that's rather generous on my part.'

'Very obliging,' with the same smile—only it had been

in place too long now and had a slightly forced look about it.

'Furthermore,' I added, 'I liked your family very much and I may see them again. I have no intention of telling them that I've met you; and if I'm ever introduced to you under their roof it will be as though we were complete strangers.'

He turned to Pérez. 'You see how considerate some North Americans can be.'

'He's a very nice man,' Pérez agreed with every appearance of sincerity. Then with a broad grin : 'And he makes us laugh.'

'Well,' I said, getting up from the creaking chair, 'the show's over for today. Don't miss next week's performance. It'll have you rolling in the aisles.'

Juan Gabaldon stood up too. 'Please don't go just yet.'

'Why not?'

'There's someone I want you to meet.'

'That's very kind of you; but I think I've had enough social activity for one day.'

'I most particularly want you to meet him,' Juan insisted.

'Bring him to the hotel,' I suggested. 'We can have a drink together.'

'He couldn't come to the hotel.'

'I'm sorry,' I said shortly; 'but I'm going now.' I waved my hand at the other two. 'Nice to have met you. Thank Rosa for me.'

I turned to go out of the door; but Juan stood in my way holding toward me, inconspicuously and almost, it seemed to me when I thought about it later, apologetically, a thin-bladed knife.

'I'd hoped it wouldn't come to this,' he said.

'I'd hoped so too,' I concurred.

34

'Please sit down again, Mr. Brandeis.'

'If you put it like that.'

It was odd but I felt no real fear. Indeed, in complying so readily with his request, it was as if I were concerned with sparing him the embarrassment of having his bluff called should I try to step past him. The truth was that I liked Juan, and Pérez and Tomás too; and therefore none of the consequences of our misunderstandings ever seemed to take a particularly sinister turn.

At the same time I was aware of possible danger in that they might inadvertently reveal some lawless scheme in which they were involved and then have to make up their minds whether or not they could trust me to keep such knowledge to myself. It was partly to save them from any clumsy slips by doing most of the talking myself and partly to show them I was in no position to take a legalistic view of things that I explained my reasons for leaving the States.

I was not certain if they believed me; but Pérez at least found the account highly diverting. When Rosa brought us more coffee, he told her that in the U.S.A. husbands could get rid of wives with a snap of their fingers and that if she ever annoyed him, he would take her there for a one-way holiday. It sent her off in shrieks of laughter.

It was getting dark now, but no one bothered to light a lamp.

'I'm sorry if I've been monopolising the conversation. Tell me something about your family,' I begged Juan.

'You mean about my sister, Ana, I suppose.'

'Not necessarily; but if you'd rather speak of her . . .'

'There's not much to say. She's very romantic. That's why she's rejected every marriage my parents have tried to arrange for her. It's also why, even though she's very interested in politics, she's quite hopeless at it.'

'Oh I like that!' I approved. 'I'm crazy about romanticism. Back in the States we've got this new invention on sale everywhere—sex I believe it's called in the trade—and it's driven romance right out of the market. Perhaps it's only in countries where traces of feudalism still linger that you get real romantics any more.'

'Now you do sound like a tourist, Mr. Brandeis—taking a holiday from the hygienic standards of life in the States to indulge briefly a romantic taste in the more primitive conditions of America's commercial colonies.'

'That's not what I mean,' I objected. 'And it's not a very happy simile—comparing your lovely sister with bad plumbing.'

Suddenly the curtain at the door was swept back and a bulky form pushed into the room. 'The stuff's come, Juan! It was landed about . . .'

'Quiet!' Juan called out a warning and jerked his head in my direction.

Horace Watson had not seen me in the dark room and he shut up at once as though someone had hit him in the stomach. He stood there for a moment or so, his face working in confusion. Then, fat arms raised in a gesture of distress: 'Why didn't you get rid of him?'

'It seemed best for El Huero to see him first. Why didn't you find out who was here before you started blurting out our business?'

'But I thought . . .' His stricken face turned toward me in the gloom and I could see from his expression that he was quite sick at his own carelessness.

'Well,' I thought with a shrug, 'the one thing I feared has happened now.' And even though it was *their* problem created by their own damned foolishness, I could not in the circumstances be very detached about it.

What 'stuff' was he talking about? I wondered. Obviously they were involved in some sort of smuggling

36

operation, possibly contraband coming across the Gulf to some point on the east coast.

But 'stuff'? I frowned. What kind of stuff would it be? And when I realised what it most likely was, I wished fervently that I had not thought of it. Dope, of course. They were probably receiving it here and then running it north. What better cover could Watson have for such traffic than that of a commercial traveller in medical drugs?

With a tremendous creaking he had lowered himself into a cane chair by the door. 'What do we do now?' he asked rather helplessly. 'About him I mean,' with a nod in my direction.

'Exactly what I was going to do before you blundered in like that.' Juan's voice had taken on a note of author-ity. 'I want El Huero to see him. El Huero's more likely to assess how innocent he is than we are.'

'I'm so innocent,' I put in quickly, 'that I haven't the least idea what you're talking about.'

No one said anything to that and there was an uneasy quiet in the room. Ominous, almost. I really was begin-ning to be worried now. Juan and the other two might be the most agreeable rogues in the world; but they were not in this alone. And, anyway, dope smuggling was a very nasty business that set its own rules, regardless of what sort of people got mixed up in it. Besides, I would not feel the same myself about drug running as I would about some scheme for cheating the customs over the tariff on watches, say. I might even find myself, to my inde-scribable horror, taking up a dangerous moral stand on the issue.

'This El Huero,' I said, and my voice did not sound altogether natural to me, 'when is he going to turn up?'

'That's the problem,' Juan shrugged. 'It might not be till tomorrow morning.'

'Won't the people at the hotel wonder what's happened to me?'

He smiled. 'They're broad minded at the *Buena Vista*. They're not likely to think anything of a tourist who stays out all night.'

'Even when meals are included in his bill?'

'He can stay here tonight?' Juan asked Pérez.

'Sí. We can put a pallet on the floor.' He turned to me. 'It won't be so comfortable, señor; but you are very welcome.'

'That's something I appreciate,' I said sarcastically— 'the warm hospitality of simple people, sharing their last crust with you.'

'We may have tamales, I think.'

Juan turned to Watson. 'There're several things I have to do in connection with the news you've brought. You'll have to stay here to keep Mr. Brandeis company.' He added: 'It's only fair under the circumstances. It may teach you to be more careful.'

'My company may not be very stimulating,' I protested; 'but it's never been described as a punishment before.'

'And suppose Mr. Brandeis gets restless during the night?' Juan asked significantly.

Watson reached in the pocket of his linen jacket shapeless with sweat. He brought out a small, snub-nosed revolver which he placed on the table beside his chair.

Juan got up and stood in front of me. 'Believe me, I regret the necessity of keeping you here. If you ever understand what's involved, I think you'll agree that there was nothing else we could do.'

'I don't want to know,' I told him. 'If you see Ana, you might explain that a visit we planned to make to some local ruins may be delayed. I only hope I don't become one myself.'

He smiled and made an amiable gesture of farewell.

Pure hypocrisy, I thought. He raised the curtain and left the house.

Pérez also got up. 'I'll tell Rosa to get us something to eat. You'd better go to the cantina, Tomás, and buy some drink.'

I was left alone with Watson. 'I knew yesterday in the hotel bar I should've told you I was holding that chair for someone else. It just doesn't pay to be polite any more.'

He grinned feebly and picked up the revolver—more to have something to do with his hands, I hoped, than out of any aggressive intention. His face was shiny with sweat and he was obviously suffering from his awareness of the stupid mistake he had made. He seemed to be afraid and that frightened me. I think I would have preferred to be guarded by a bully than someone who might do something foolish out of fear.

'Please relax,' I begged. 'I haven't the most remote idea of making the slightest move.'

'It isn't that.' He shook his head miserably. 'You don't know how much is at stake.'

'And I don't want to,' I said again.

'It's so important I don't want to mess things up.'

'I don't want you to, either. Tell me, Watson, was it an accident you took that chair opposite me in the hotel?'

'I was curious about you; and then, later, when you seemed to know Señor Gabaldon . . .'

'I see.' Below the level at which I had felt a certain disquiet at the way these new acquaintances of mine played about with knives and pistols and rather arbitrarily disposed of my time, something else had been troubling me even more. All sorts of apparently accidental happenings, about which I thought nothing as they occurred, kept turning out to be part of a pattern—but a pattern whose fabrication I had no part in. It was all beginning to seem fatal in the most literal sense. I felt I could scarcely make any move at all, however inconsequential, without its fitting into a deliberate plan devised behind my back, as it were; and even if this awareness turned me stubborn and made me refuse to budge, that, too, might prove to be what was required of me in terms of some scheme of which I was ignorant.

A kind of superstitious awe not only touched the events of the immediate past; but stretched back further into my life. When I had decided several years earlier to write about the work of a revolutionary Latin American poet, I had thought it was a literary whim on my part—or, at most, a way of cocking a snook at the right-wing witch-hunters in the States. But that no longer seemed to be the case. Nothing seemed casually fortuitous any more.

Perhaps, I reflected gloomily, such a fate overtook everyone at some stage or other—all the random events of his life suddenly seeming to be caught up together in a very tight little design bearing no resemblance whatsoever to anything he had actually proposed himself.

This oppressive train of thought was interrupted by Watson's shifting heavily in his chair.

'Don't just sit there staring at me like that,' he said.

'Of course not,' I responded hastily. 'What shall we talk about? It's—er, it's been hot today, hasn't it?'

3

'It's Nice to be Trusted'

AFTER a scratch meal consisting mostly of beans, I made myself as comfortable as possible on the lumpy pallet. I must have been tired because I soon dropped off to sleep to wake at cock crow—which was not surprising since the cock was in the same room with me.

I watched it pecking at the earth floor between the massive legs of Watson, still snoring in the chair which had been fitted out with pillows for his night's rest. Before going to sleep I had practically put myself on parole by assuring him that I had no intention of wandering off in the dark. The idea of a sleepy Watson hanging over me all night with a pistol in his hands had not appealed to me at all.

Throwing back the serape I got up and walked out into the little courtyard at the back of the house. The air was cool and fresh and so clear that that mountains seemed to begin just beyond the rusty barbed wire fence. Chickens clucked at my feet and from somewhere down the dusty street a woman's voice was raised in domestic scolding. I filled my lungs with the fresh air, looking up into the cloudless sky where several buzzards wheeled in effortless flight.

I turned at a sound to see Watson as he came out of the house. 'It's been arranged for you to meet El Huero this morning,' he said. 'Maybe we can get this thing cleared up.'

'I hope so.'

Pérez beckoned from the door and gave me a bowl of hot water. There was an old-fashioned straight-edged razor laid out as well, in case my appearance was important enough to me to risk cutting my throat.

We ate some stale tortillas washed down with black coffee; and then Pérez led me out to the aged Ford parked in the front yard.

I got in and said to Watson, who stood there with his wrinkled coat pulled down on the side where the revolver was pocketed: 'Nice day for a picnic. Aren't you coming?'

'Too much to do here. I may see you later.'

We waited till Tomás arrived and climbed into the back. Pérez twisted a piece of baling wire around the door on his side to keep it closed and started the engine. We bucked out of the yard with a series of chicken-scattering explosions and turned into the dirt road which led out of town.

This road crossed the little spring-fed stream by a stone bridge and zig-zagged up toward the notch of Silla Pass. The old car was barely moving by the time we got to the top. We willed it over the last few feet and then picked up speed on the other side.

I laughed and Pérez turned toward me with a grin. 'She's very old, señor. Someday she won't be able to get over the Pass and I'll have to shoot her, I think.'

'I was considering my efforts to get away from Americans,' I explained my wry amusement. 'It's just occurred to me that I may never see *any* of them again.'

'You will, señor—soon.'

'This man, El Huero, what's he like?'

'Oh, a man much like yourself.'

'I doubt that. Why is he called "El Huero"?'

'His hair's like yours, señor—very blond.'

'I suppose that *is* a bit unusual.'

Pérez shrugged. 'Many North Americans have hair like that.'

'You mean he's a gringo?'

'Sí,' Pérez laughed.

This news upset me. I had been imagining a Pancho Villa type bandido with a rough sense of humour and a shrewd knowledge of men who would soon realise that I was absolutely harmless and, after a couple of drinks of mescal, send me on my way. I had to dismantle this carefully-constructed image and replace it with that of a flaxen-haired, cold-eyed mobster from the North who would gun down mercilessly anyone who might expose the racket he was running down here.

'Tell me, Pérez—are you afraid of this El Huero?'

'Why should I be afraid? We're on the same side.'

'Yes. That makes a difference.'

On this side of the ridge the valley was very different from the shallow basin in which San Pedro nestled. No springs quickened a softer vegetation, no canals supported trees or shrubs. Nothing but cactus grew among the huge tumbled rocks through which the dusty road made its tortuous way. We bumped along for perhaps an hour leaving clouds of dust behind us; and then Pérez turned off the road and we drove down the dry bed of an arroyo for another mile or so till the way was blocked by boulders.

Here we stopped and got out. I followed Pérez and Tomás up a winding track which climbed to a rock shelf jutting out from high red sandstone cliffs. Perched on this shelf was a wooden shack which looked out over the desolate valley where we could still see the streamers of dust churned up by our approach.

Two men, Mexican by their dress, were sitting in the shade beside the door. They waved languidly as we came up; and one of them got slowly to his feet and stuck his head inside the room. He turned and motioned for me to

enter. Pérez and Tomás squatted on the hard packed earth
with their backs to the wall as I stepped inside.

There were only two tiny windows high up and the
light from one of them slanted down dramatically on a
man standing behind a crudely-made table which, with
several battered chairs, was all the furniture in the room.
He was solidly-built, about thirty-five, with a shock of very
fair hair and a broad, strong-jawed face so deeply freckled
that he appeared to have a solid coat of tan as dark as any
Indian.

I must have been under considerable tension. When I
had briefly studied those grey eyes with the skin crinkling
good-humouredly at the corners and that wide pleasantly
smiling mouth, I let out an audible sigh of relief.

He poured water from a bag hanging by the table and
pushed the cup toward me. 'Sit down,' he invited in a
resonant voice. 'You're Kyle Brandeis?'

'That's right,' taking the chair nearest the table. 'Cigarette?' I held out a packet and he accepted one.

He looked me over during the time it took us to inhale
a couple of times and fill the shaft of light with eddying
smoke. 'Well,' he said, 'you've got rather tangled up with
us, haven't you?'

'The whole thing's a mistake,' I assured him.

'Very likely; but it's unfortunate all the same.'

'What's a night on a lumpy mattress!' I said with a
shrug. 'I'm willing to forget the whole thing.'

'That's not what I meant,' he laughed; 'and you know
it.'

'I know very little. I want it to stay like that. You see,
the longer I'm kept hanging around the more I'm going to
find out—however much I try not to. You ought to tell
your people to get rid of me while I'm still at the stage of
only being able to make the wildest conjectures as to
what's going on.'

'Get rid of you?' He raised his sandy eyebrows.

'Turn me loose would've been a happier way of putting it.'

He drummed on the table with his stubby fingers. 'Tell me about these wild conjectures of yours.'

'Why can't I keep my big mouth shut!' I exclaimed in exasperation with myself.

'That's what worries *us*,' he said amiably enough.

'I was trying to be honest with you. If I denied speculating at all about why I should've been detained, you'd know I was lying.'

'If you were all that honest, you'd have threatened us with complaining to the police.'

'Well, I'm honest enough to admit that I have personal reasons for not wishing to do so—which ought to suit you very well.'

He leaned back in his chair and regarded me thoughtfully. 'We're not getting anywhere, are we?'

'Apparently not.'

'I'd like to approach this in a different way, if you'll bear with me. Would you mind answering some questions?'

'Go ahead. I'll let you know if you come to one I don't like the sound of.'

'When you first began your literary review you were lecturing in English literature at Columbia University, not long after coming over from England. Correct?'

'That's right. You can go to the head of the class.'

'Did you know a man on the faculty called Jason McComber?'

'I did. He was in the law department.'

'What happened to him when he left the university and began practising?'

'He achieved some notoriety taking up the cases of those who fell foul of the UnAmerican Activities Committee.'

'Did you remain friendly with him?'

'Naturally. I liked him. I admired the stand he took. And I wasn't at all sure I wouldn't need his services some day.'

'Do you remember some of the people he defended?'

'What is this?' I objected.

'I know what I'm doing,' he told me. 'Please answer my question.'

'Well, let's see. All this was some years ago. There was the Bartlett passport case. Joe Bartlett was a member of the Communist Party. I knew him slightly because we'd been on one or two committees together. Then there was the contempt of court case brought against Sammy Ekhardt. And, of course, Barry Jones . . .'

'What had Barry Jones done?' the man interrupted me.

'Nothing illegal. But I think he was a Party member too; and he'd certainly been responsible for organising the fruit-pickets in California, mostly Mexican labourers. So, the Committee was gunning for him—not without a bit of pushing from Californian land-owners, I suspect.'

'Would you know Jones if you saw him?'

'No I don't suppose I would.'

He leaned forward with a smile. 'I'm Barry Jones.'

'You!'

'Yes. After McComber got me off the hook, I moved around the States for a while, finding it difficult to get work, and finally I drifted south.'

'Well, I'll be damned.' I stood up and reached across the table. 'I'd like to shake your hand. I can still recall the way you told off some of those congressmen.'

'Thanks,' gripping my hand firmly in his.

'Tell me,' sitting down again, 'how did all this El Huero business start?'

'It was a nickname given me by my Mexican friends in

46

California. It followed me when I came down here.'

'Well I'm damned,' I could only repeat. 'You know, this is quite an occasion for me. You were something of a hero of mine. We intellectuals tend to have a thing, anyway, about working-class leaders in the thick of the fray; and I always wondered, if it ever came to the crunch, whether I'd be able to stand up to them with anything like your courage and dignity.'

'Cut it out,' he protested. 'You'll have me unable to get my sombrero on—and in this climate you need one.'

'There's only one thing,' I frowned. 'You've told me a good deal about yourself; but I can't see what you've found out about me.'

'More than you probably realise. But I haven't finished yet.'

'Fire away, El Huero.'

'Call me Barry.'

'Sure; and I'd be Kyle to my friends—if I had any.'

'Haven't you any—Kyle?'

'No. I've collected wives instead. I have wives like some people have mice.'

'Oh? How many would you say, at a rough estimate?'

'Well, two. I know that sounds like an anti-climax; but only if you haven't met the particular specimens I collected. Both of them eat like a regiment and spend money like a boatload of drunken sailors.'

He grinned. 'We all have our crosses, Kyle.'

'But mine are double.'

He drummed some more on the table and then those searching grey eyes met mine again. 'How much do you know about Manuel Ortiz?'

'I'm glad you brought that up; because it's caused a certain amount of confusion. Several years ago, for no particular reason, I wrote an article about his poetry which...'

47

'I read it.'

'Then you know that it was a purely literary exercise like all the other things I do for the *Western Review*.'

'If you think that, then you don't know yourself very well. What came across in that piece was a deep sympathy for the revolutionary content of the poems and a passionate protest at man's injustice to man.'

'Well, I don't deny that I may have *some* feelings about liberation struggles. I mean, you take a man bound hand and foot to a couple of cannibalistic viragos . . .'

He shook his head. 'It won't do, Kyle.'

'Won't it?'

'No. You've got much finer feelings than you like to admit—not out of modesty of course. You're dodging the demands those feelings might make on you.'

'There may be something in that,' I was prepared to agree. 'We lower middle-class intellectuals are a pretty corrupt lot, basically. We may get fired by the right ideas; but when it comes to a choice between them and our creature comforts . . .'

'That won't do, either,' he shook his head again—'trying to take refuge behind the characteristics of your class.'

'Let's get back to Ortiz,' I suggested. 'It's true I was interested in his work; but that had nothing to do with this trip to Central America.'

'However, since you *are* here and he *is* locked up in a prison on the outskirts of the capital, do you intend making any effort at all to see him?'

'Well,' I hesitated, 'that's a proposition Señor Gabaldon put to me. If it could be arranged—yes, I suppose I would like to visit the old boy. He's a great man and there aren't so many of those about these days.'

'More than you probably realise,' Jones said firmly. 'They aren't all so well known as Manuel Ortiz; but they exist all right.'

'I wouldn't exclude you from such a list,' I told him frankly.

'I wasn't thinking of that. I was thinking of the many people of this country, most of whom can't even read or write, who're capable of greatness and will prove it when history sets the stage for them.'

'I'm sure you're right. I simply haven't had your opportunities of working with them—not of course that you haven't made those opportunities yourself.'

'What I mean,' he said with some embarrassment at my frank admiration, 'is that the greatness of Ortiz consists in seeing that potential greatness in the ordinary people of this land. That's what his love for them is based on.'

'No doubt. And their love for *him* is a demonstration of that greatness in themselves.'

'Exactly.' He got up from the table and moved about the room restlessly.

I had been aware of a growing excitement behind that strong, impassive countenance. But then all I had heard of the man told me there must be times when his political convictions burned with such a clear bright flame that they lit up brilliantly from within that solid, four-square shape.

He turned toward me and stood, legs slightly straddled, hands clasped behind, as though he were settling himself firmly on a line he had just decided upon.

'I started questioning you, Kyle Brandeis, just as I had been instructed to—in order to find out if we could safely let you go and forget about you. But there came a time in my interrogation, without my really knowing it, when I was trying to find out something else—whether we could safely ask you to join us.'

'Join you in what?' I enquired cautiously.

'Why in freeing Ortiz of course.'

49

'Bringing pressure to bear on the government to release him you mean?'

'I do not,' Jones stated with finality. 'Would you expect
to find me involved in an attempt to prove that a government under U.S. influence is more liberal than people
might have supposed?'

'Perhaps not.'

'Look, Kyle. Whoever's responsible for getting Ortiz
out of jail is going to make considerable political capital
out of it. Isn't that so? Well, to whom should that credit
belong? Wouldn't you say to the people who love him?
Shouldn't *they* be the ones to secure his freedom?'

'I suppose so.'

'That's what I'm thinking we should ask you to join—a
popular movement to *force* the bars of that prison and set
Ortiz free.'

'I see.'

'That's the whole beauty of it. We don't go on our knees
and beg corrupt administrators to release that great poet
out of pity. We don't collect the signatures of a lot of
patronising liberal writers in the States who've probably
never read a line he's written.'

'Quite a few who signed the petition I launched were
under the mistaken impression that he was a Hungarian
freedom fighter,' I admitted ruefully.

'We don't do any of those things because we know that
the enemy can't be defeated by his own means. To try to
use liberal institutions to achieve our ends would be like
trying to cheat a card-sharper. No, Kyle,' shaking his
head as a teacher might at a slightly backward pupil, 'we
march on that prison like an army with banners and
batter down the walls of political injustice.'

'Do you mind if the banner I carry is a white flag? I
suspect there'll be some guards around that prison—
with guns.'

'I don't mean literally of course.' Barry Jones returned to the table and sat down. 'We want to win this skirmish with the government as economically as possible. We'll even stoop to low cunning if it suits our purpose best.'

'I might be helpful there,' I conceded.

'You might be very helpful indeed,' he took me up. 'You can move around quite freely and no one's going to pay any attention to you. No one's going to be suspicious even if you demand an interview with Ortiz. Your known interest in his work would make it seem perfectly natural. We might be able to get a message to him through you.'

'As to that . . .'

'There's nobody else, Kyle. There're extradition orders for me all over Central America. And of course none of the people I'm in contact with here could get anywhere near Ortiz.'

'Have you got many of them working for you?' I asked by way of changing the subject.

'They don't work *for* me. We're all in it together.'

'Sure. But I assumed you were probably the main . . .'

'Well I'm not,' with that same finality. 'I serve this venture on exactly the same terms as Juan Gabaldon or Pérez who brought you here. We have our leaders of course—appointed by us. That's why I can only ask if you're *willing* to join us. I can't say whether you'd be accepted as one of us or not.'

'Don't I know rather a lot now *not* to be accepted?'

'Very little you could prove. I admit that if you did know too much and yet weren't really considered acceptable, it might be awkward.'

'No, you're absolutely right,' I hastened to say. 'There's not one damned thing I could prove; and I'd look pretty silly going to the authorities with no evidence whatsoever, wouldn't I? Besides, what would be the point of it? I mean, what would be in it for me? Not that the question

of personal gain has ever so much as crossed my mind; but
only that I'm on your side in this business. I mean, hell, I'd
like to see Ortiz freed. Whatever gave you the idea I
wouldn't? Of course I know you have to be very careful
in a game like this; but you can't afford to have no faith
in others at all, can you? In fact, the more I think of it
the more convinced I become that any suspicions you're
entertaining are unworthy of you, Barry. You, as much
as any man I know, must realise that you've got to trust
people in order to be trusted yourself. I believe you'll
find when the chips are down, that I'm a man to cross
the river with—always providing it isn't too deep.'

He laughed good humouredly. 'You've covered the
question pretty thoroughly—my side of it as well as yours.'

'I like to keep the record straight.'

'You're all right, Kyle. I believe this is going to work
out fine.'

I felt flattered and probably showed it. I was not very
enthusiastic about getting involved; but I had begun to
doubt that I'd ever really be left alone till they had got
Ortiz out of the cooler. In any case, I was only committed to a vague willingness to help; and if they checked
up on me at all, they were bound to discover how completely unqualified I was for anything in the least desperate. In fact, if they were smart, they would merely impli-
cate me to the extent of keeping me quiet.

Barry Jones got up to indicate that we had taken the
matter as far as we could at present. 'You'll be hearing
from us.'

'Here?' I asked.

He shrugged. 'Here or somewhere.'

I glanced around the ramshackle hut with raised eyebrows.

'I don't stay here,' he explained. 'It's a useful meeting

point between San Pedro and our headquarters back in the mountains.'

I got up too. 'What do I do now?'

'Wait till you hear from us.'

'Where do I wait?'

'At your hotel—wherever you like.'

'I'm free then?'

'Completely,' adding with a grin : 'You've got to trust people in order to be trusted yourself, haven't you?'

'Right.' I held out my hand and he shook it with a firm grip. 'I consider it an honour to have met you, Barry. I've heard such a lot about you.'

'Oh we'll get along fine,' he said modestly.

We went outside and Pérez and Tomás got to their feet.

'You can take him back to the hotel,' Jones told them.

'It's a pleasure,' Pérez said. 'He's our friend.'

'I make them laugh,' I explained.

'I don't know of a better basis for friendship.'

We started down the steep path. When I looked back, Barry Jones was still watching and he gave me a cheery wave.

Bumping back toward town, I suddenly realised that there were a lot of things I might have asked if I had thought about them at the time. I wondered how Watson had got mixed up in this scheme and whether Jones shared my distrust of the man. It was also puzzling that after such elaborate precautions during the night to keep me prisoner I should now be released just as if I enjoyed their fullest confidence. I could not understand why it had not occurred to me to put such questions—except that Barry Jones was a bit of a spellbinder. Still, the very fact that he was involved in all this made me feel that it must be all right.

We drove up to the hotel and under the curious stares

of the other guests I got out and bid an amiable farewell to Pérez and Tomás, promising to pay them an unenforced visit as soon as I could.

I went up to my room to wash before lunch. My suitcase was open on the bed. I rushed to it and looked inside the flap. My passport was gone and so were my traveller's cheques. There was a note, though. 'We'll keep these things for you,' it read. 'You won't need them for a while.'

'Nice to be trusted,' I muttered sarcastically to myself as I went into the bathroom and dashed cold water on my face. 'My reward, no doubt, for trusting others.'

4

'I May be Falling in Love'

IN THE midst of lunch I suddenly stopped eating and
with fork suspended said to myself : 'Horace Watson
of course!'—meaning that it must have been Watson who
had taken my passport.

I wanted it back. If I *did* decide to help in some scheme
for releasing Ortiz, it must be because it was my own
choice and not because they had brought pressure to bear
on me. I did not believe for an instant that Barry Jones
would have approved of such methods. My passport had
been taken before the results of my interview with him
could have been known. But I could not be sure that he
would have the final word on the question of allowing
me to come in with them freely if at all.

I dabbed at my mouth with my napkin and pushed my
chair back.

'Too hot for you?' my table companion asked in a mid-
western accent while pointing at my unfinished meal with
his knife.

'I'm one of those people things are always too hot for,'
I explained.

At the reception desk I asked for the number of
Watson's room and was also handed an envelope which
had been left there for me. I put it in my pocket and
crossed the patio to a stairway leading up to an inner
balcony onto which Watson's room opened.

He was inside and at my brief rap invited me to enter.

'Oh it's you,' he said looking up from the cane chair in

55

which he sprawled. His shirt was open and beads of sweat glistened in the fat folds of his neck. 'Want a drink?' He flapped a podgy hand toward the bottles and ice bucket on the table beside his chair.

'Don't disturb yourself,' I urged unnecessarily. 'I'll make it.'

'This climate's going to kill me,' he complained—'unless some guy down here gets to me first.'

It sounded melodramatic and I did not comment. Straightening with the glass cold against my palm, I asked him directly : 'Where is it, Watson?'

'Where's what?'

'My goddamned passport.'

His surprise seemed genuine. 'How would I know? I've enough trouble keeping track of my own stuff.'

I brought out the slip of paper. 'You don't know who left me this?'

He read the note which I held before him and shook his head. 'There're some funny things going on around here.' And then : 'What happened when you saw El Huero?'

'We got along fine.' I sat down in a chair opposite him.

'So he bought your story that the whole thing was a misunderstanding?'

'That's right.'

Watson frowned deeply.

'You still don't believe it?' I asked.

'It's not that. If El Huero and the other big shots figure it's all right, who am I to complain? What beats me is that a stranger turns up and seems to know more than is healthy. I report the matter in good faith and what happens?'

'I don't know. What does happen?'

'They begin to distrust *me*.'

'So you got ticked off for mentioning your suspicions?

Well, I'm sorry; but it's hardly my fault.'

'Whether you meant to or not, you've made a fool of
me. You see,' looking at me resentfully, 'they don't have a
very high opinion of me anyway. They think I'm only in
it for the money.'

'In what? Getting Ortiz free?'

'If you don't know, you wouldn't expect me to tell you.'

'You nearly did yesterday when you busted into Pérez'
place.'

'I know. That was stupid. I hope Juan hasn't said anything about it. But,' shaking his head rather sorrowfully,
'in this sort of racket you never know who you can trust.'

'Then you can scarcely expect them to trust *you*, can
you?'

'It's not the same, though. I've been at it a long time
now and I've never handled a job I didn't believe in. Sure
I get a commission. A man's got to live; but I've knocked
back plenty of deals I could've made good money on.' He
seemed very eager for me to accept him as a man of integrity. 'In the circles I move in they know that about me.
I've got a good reputation in the trade, you know.'

'That's fine,' I told him. 'The next time I drop into my
corner drug store I'll put in a good word for you.'

He took no notice of my jibe. Lifting his glass he finished
his drink; and then, with another slow shake of his head:
'There's been something kind of funny about this one all
along.'

'Since I haven't any idea what you're talking about . . .'

'I wonder if that's true,' focussing his gaze on me. 'Who
in the hell *are* you working for, Brandeis?'

'Nobody at all—except maybe a couple of over-blown
females back in the States.'

'I wish I could believe that.'

'I don't see why you don't. The man you call El Huero
whom I know as Barry Jones believes it. He's even asked

me if I'd be willing to help pull off this scheme they've
got for springing Ortiz.'

'Is that so! You see, it's just like I said. They seem to
trust everybody but me.'

'It's my frank, open countenance,' I assured him. 'One
look at me and people just know I'm not clever enough
to get away with anything.'

'Of course the Ortiz business is only part of it.'

'Well, since they all seem to trust me, why don't you try
trusting me too, and tell me the rest of it.'

I apparently touched some chord. 'I wish to Christ
I could!' he exclaimed fervently. 'I need to talk to *some-
body* about it. I think,' raising his eyes to mine, 'I think
I'm in trouble.'

'That can happen,' I said philosophically, 'in the kind
of game you're in.'

'I don't mean the Federales. Trouble with the police
you expect. No,' letting his head sink again gloomily, 'it's
something else. This job doesn't smell right. In my business you get a feeling for these things.'

'Can't you get out of it?'

'Sure. I could take my cut and vamoose. But like I was
telling you, it isn't just the money. I take an interest in
whether things work out all right. I guess it's like what
in other businesses they call aftersales servicing.'

I was beginning to feel a little sorry for him—with a
certain wary reserve in case he was only playing on my
sympathy. It would be the easiest thing in the world for
one of them to pretend to be at odds with the others in
order to find out what I really thought about it all. And
yet Watson did look rather pathetic. If I found it difficult
to like or respect the man, perhaps others did too; and
with the best will in the world he could not get himself
accepted as a worthy confederate.

'I don't suppose . . .' he began hopefully and then broke off.

'What?'

'Nothing.'

'Go on. You were going to ask some favour of me. I can only say no.'

He rubbed his hand over his face in perplexity. 'I guess it'd seem too much like I didn't trust them.'

'Still, if you think they don't trust *you* . . .'

'That's right. And, anyway, if they're prepared to let you in on this thing, I don't see why I shouldn't get you to help me carry out my part of it.'

'I'm not promising anything. You'd better tell me what you want me to do.'

'You don't have to *do* anything. I've got to drive to the coast tomorrow to make some arrangements. I don't know the people I'm supposed to meet there. Once I leave San Pedro, I could disappear for good and nobody'd ever know what happened to me. So,' pausing before he finally brought it out, 'I'd like you to come along with me—just for the ride.'

'I don't know about that, Watson.'

'You're afraid to get mixed up with me, in case they decide you aren't reliable either.'

'It's not that. I didn't say I'd actually come in on this thing. All I said was that they'd asked me if I was *willing* to join in with them. I don't know that I am. And even if I were, they might not all agree about accepting me.'

'You didn't tell me that before,' he protested. 'You sort of gave me the idea that you enjoyed El Huero's confidence.'

'Maybe I do, but he's not the only one who has a say and I'm not sure I want to get involved at all.'

I burst out laughing at his look of resentment.

'What's so funny?'

'Your practically accusing me of deceit. That's rather amusing under the circumstances. And what's even more amusing is my allowing you to put me in the wrong over it. I'm like that, though. Some thug trying to steal my wallet could complain that I didn't hold my jaw at the right angle for him to hit it and I'd apologise without thinking.'

'I'm not a thug.'

'I didn't say you were.'

'Then you won't come with me?'

'I don't think so. I'm sorry.'

'Well,' shrugging, 'I guess I can't blame you. I'll just have to go through with it on my own. I suppose I always knew it'd catch up with me sooner or later.'

'You'll be all right,' I tried to cheer him up. 'I think you're letting your imagination get the better of you.'

'I wish that were true,' he said. 'The trouble is—I know I haven't got much imagination.'

I left him sitting there, brooding over another drink he had mixed for himself.

What I should have been doing was writing something pretty *recherché* for the next issue of the *Western Review*. I had an idea for an article showing that the only way a critic could deal appropriately with a work intended by the author to communicate a sense of the incommunicability of individual experience was by leaving the page absolutely blank; but I was not sure how to present this project to the printers.

Anyway, when I returned to my room I did not feel like writing, or even leaving pages blank. My recent whiffs of something a bit more exciting than propping up a tired journal had put me in one of those moods when the whole profession of letters seemed like talking about life behind its back.

The reference to letters put me in mind of the envelope

I had put in my pocket before going to see Watson. I opened it and found a brief note from Ana Gabaldon mentioning that she had called at the hotel to show me around the town.

That settled it, then. The article could be done tomorrow. After all, I shrugged, when in Rome . . .

I had a shower and dressed, even running to a rather gaudy red tie which went well with my inflamed eyes from a restless night on that lumpy pallet.

The sun was well down the sky when I left the hotel; but it was still hot and very few sounds of life drifted up from the town. The front of the cathedral looked like ornately-worked gold; the deserted central plaza shimmering in the heat seemed to be awash with liquid gold; and a warm gold glow coated the buildings of adobe. It was probably not a reasonable hour to call; but I could always plead a foreigner's ignorance of local customs. I turned in through the iron gateway, blinked in the glare thrown back from the white walls of the Gabaldon hacienda and banged on the knocker.

The door was opened by Ana herself.

'I wanted to thank you for returning my call,' I explained. 'Also to express my regret for not being in and to mention that I'm free for a sight-seeing tour of San Pedro this evening. I might say, as well, that I've been thinking about your father's suggestion and have decided that I will try to get permission to see Manuel Ortiz. Furthermore . . .'

'Just a minute,' holding up her hand in protest. 'Which of all these reasons for coming here is the real one?'

'Whichever is most likely to get me past the front door. It's the multi-product approach used on housewives back in the States.'

'It's a subject you must know a lot about—housewives.'

'It's a knowledge I'd just as soon not have picked up.'

'Do come in,' she smiled. 'I think I'll accept your invitation to go down to the town. My father's resting and you can talk to him when we get back.'

'Splendid. As you perfectly well know that's just what I intended. The rest was merely to have some excuse to fall back on.'

'It seems a little over-cautious, Mr. Brandeis, when I'd already taken the step of asking for you at the hotel.'

'By never taking anything for granted I've saved myself a lot of rebuffs.'

'You must have a very sensitive nature.'

'Very. It places a great responsibility on the people I'm with—not that it's ever seemed to bother them much.'

'I'll do a few things and be with you shortly.' She pointed to the sitting room. 'Will you wait for me in there?'

'No. I'll go back to the hotel and close a deal with the old man who owns that ancient victoria which is propping up what looks vaguely like a horse between the shafts. I've been dickering with him on the off chance that you might spend the evening with me. Pick you up in twenty minutes—if that horse is merely sleeping and hasn't actually expired.'

'All right. I've wondered about that horse myself.'

I was waiting beside the carriage when she came out, dressed in something white and cool which suited me as well as it did her. I took out a handkerchief and slapped at the dusty seat before helping her up. Climbing in beside her I gestured to the old man who had watched us install ourselves somewhat gingerly in his creaking conveyance. 'Let her rip,' I said, with a dubious glance at the patched material protecting us from the sun.

Eventually the horse broke into a shambling walk and I leaned back to enjoy the ride into town. Five minutes later we had almost left behind us the gates of her house.

'Just the vehicle,' I observed, 'for a cicerone with a bad speech impediment.'

'Blonde or brunette, Mr. Brandeis?'

'I don't quite follow.'

'I was wondering what had attracted you away from the hotel when I came by there yesterday.'

'Oh, blonde. About my height and built on the lines of a heavily-armoured tank. I like to get my money's worth.'

'I think I may know whom you mean.'

'Don't you feel,' trying to change the subject, 'that calling me "Mr. Brandeis" is a little formal? Particularly when we've already reached the stage of your prying into my private life.'

'But I didn't . . .'

'The name's Kyle, Ana.'

'But I had no intention of prying. I wanted to talk to you about Juan.'

'Now you've done it!' I said in exasperation.

'Done what?'

'Spoiled this beautiful illusion I've been working on. The moment I read your note I assumed it must be something to do with your brother. But I preferred to think it was because you found me—well, interesting. I was looking forward to another pleasant hour or so of kidding myself along before you blew the whole thing sky high.'

'I'm sorry.'

'That's all right. It wasn't a very well-grounded illusion, anyway. I don't even find me very interesting, myself.'

'I *do*, as a matter of fact.'

'Thank you, Ana. I never consider a compliment worthwhile unless I've really sweated blood for it.'

By this time we had reached the first houses of town, a few hundred yards below the Gabaldon residence. 'This,' with a wave at the practically stationary buildings on

either side of the cobbled road, 'must have a great thera-
peutic value for us speed-crazed Anglo-Saxons. I'd sentence every tourist coming south to an hour a day in a
carriage like this—not just for the spiritual mortification
of moving at a snail's pace, either. Untired wheels on
cobblestones are probably very good for one's ganglia.'

'You're avoiding the subject I wanted to talk to you
about,' she accused.

'There,' I admitted, 'you've put your finger on my
most essential characteristic—an ability to dodge issues.
Life's always trying to manœuvre me into a position
where I'll have no alternative to a fairly straightforward
course of action; but I have this remarkable talent for
muddling up the simplest situation and escaping in the
general confusion.'

'You're doing it now.'

'I know. But it's not what you think, Ana. It isn't that
I don't want to help. I just don't want you to find out
yet that I can't. That would wind up our evening together before it even got started.'

She just perceptibly shook her head. 'It's *your* view of
the matter that my only reason for seeing you is to find
out about my brother.'

I looked at her sceptically. 'Now you're trying to get
around me. You shouldn't you know—not because it
wouldn't be all too easy; but because it wouldn't be necessary if I knew anything to tell you.'

She made a face at me. 'Don't you find that having
such a poor opinion of yourself tends to be self-defeating.'

'Defeat at one's own hand is so much easier to bear.'

'Well, I don't think it's that at all. I think you like to be
left alone so you make yourself out as unattractive as
possible.'

'If that's true, you're very clever, Ana. If not, you're

64

even cleverer. Could we talk about someone else for a while?'

'Juan?'

'I was going to suggest you.'

'There's so little to say,' she shrugged.

'I believe I could wax fairly eloquent on the subject; but I'll wait for a more propitious occasion.' I peered around us. 'Shouldn't you, as guide, be deciding where we're going? Another three or four hours of this spanking pace and we'll have come out on the far side of town.'

'What do you have in mind?'

I was thinking of some cool patio with a fountain where we could have a drink and talk of such vital matters as what we were going to do about dinner. Secluded and quiet of course, with a hospedero who shot tourists on sight unless they were accompanied by a native. 'Oh, anything you say.'

She leaned forward and gave directions to the old man. We turned down a side street and stopped in front of an entrance I would have been unable to distinguish from a private dwelling.

I tried to pay off the old man; but he waved his hand and insisted that he was at our disposal for the whole evening.

We went inside and I exclaimed: 'Uncanny!'

'Why?'

'You've conjured up exactly what I was thinking about. You must be a mind-reader.'

She looked at me speculatively. 'Not a very good one.'

'That's all right. I haven't a very good mind.'

We sat at a table near the fountain and I ordered drinks.

'Very pleasant,' I said. And then with a frown: 'Something's been puzzling me. What makes you think I know anything about Juan?'

'I believe you're in contact with someone who's involved in the same business.'

'Maybe.'

'I don't trust him.'

'Watson? Neither do I.'

'I meant the one they call El Huero.'

'Now wait a minute, Ana. Is this an example of feminine intuition? If so, I don't think much of it. El Huero's the only one in all this I know anything about.'

'What do you know about him?'

'He's been locked up for organising Mexican labourers in California for one thing. He was hounded all during the McCarthy period. He's a man of the greatest courage and determination. In fact, if I'd had anything at all to do with the shaping of Kyle Brandeis I'd have made him as much like El Huero as possible.'

'But don't you see—anyone who was secretly working with reactionary forces would have to establish a reputation like that.'

'Sure,' I laughed. 'That sounds all right. But if you carry it to its logical conclusion we'd have to suppose that the general secretary of the CPUSA was really an FBI agent.'

'How do you know he's not?'

'And J. Edgar Hoover? He must be a very successful communist spy, wouldn't you say?'

'You can make fun of me as much as you like. All I can say is that I hope no one as naive as you ever gets mixed up in espionage.'

'I've no intention of doing so. And I'm not making fun of you, Ana. It's just—well, according to your line of reasoning one would have to suppose that Manuel Ortiz himself was carrying out a very elaborate deception.'

'That's different. I *know* Tio Manuel.'

'Have another drink.'

'I haven't finished this one. Order another one for yourself and we'll probably come out even.'

'Now you're trying to get me drunk,' I said as I beckoned to the waiter. 'I'd have every excuse for thinking *you're* a beautiful spy sent to trap me.'

'It may be your safest course,' she answered with a smile.

We finished our drinks and went outside. The sun had gone down but it was still light. I could see the twin towers of the cathedral above the house opposite and I suggested that we walk to the central plaza.

We set forth afoot with the old man following us in the victoria.

'Not too fast,' I told her. 'We don't want to leave our equipage so far behind it gets lost altogether.'

In the plaza people were strolling about on the pavement and in one corner a group was listening to a little band of musicians playing a sentimental tune. We sat on a bench under a palm tree and watched the sky darken and a sickle moon light up over the cathedral.

The musicians came over to us with their guitars and trumpets and offered to play anything we liked. We tested their repertoire with various suggestions and, after a while, when we got up to stroll about the plaza ourselves, they followed us, still playing. The old man in the coach whipped his horse into slow motion and kept up with us as well. Some children who had been rushing about the plaza trying to cadge pennies to buy ices also joined in the procession.

We came to a corner of the plaza and I turned to give arm signals to the host behind us, indicating that I intended to execute a left wheel.

'All we need is the San Pedro fire department,' I told her, 'and we'd have a mass rising on our hands. In fact, we could march on the capital and bring down the government if they didn't let Uncle Manuel out.'

I had kept her hand in mine after helping her to her feet and we sauntered on, fingers interlaced. Guitars and trumpets accompanied us with one of those sweet Latin American songs that has a melancholy catch in it and the rhythmic plodding of the tired old horse beat out the time while the delighted shrieks of the little boys interjected a dithyrambic note.

I looked up at the thin slice of moon, breathed deeply the flower-scented air and let the combination of sounds wash around my ears. 'You know,' I said to her, 'I may be falling in love. But don't look so startled. It's possibly nothing more specific than this land itself which is the object of my burgeoning passion.'

It seemed a shame to break up the parade; but we were getting hungry. Opposite a little restaurant Ana pointed out to me, we made a dash for it and disappeared to the cheerful huzzahs of our many camp followers.

Not till we were having coffee after an excellent meal did she come back to the subject which was on her mind.

'Juan is so impulsive,' she said.

'So I've noticed.'

'But it isn't only that. You see, he resents his background very much. That's what's been making trouble between him and Papa—almost as if our parents had played a dirty trick on him by giving him the stigma of our class at birth. He feels that no one can take him seriously as a revolutionary; and I'm afraid he'll be driven into reckless and dangerous actions to try to prove himself.'

'Have you talked to him about it?'

'Oh he won't listen to me! He says I'll never do anything but *dream* about a liberated country. When I've tried to tell him he ought to be more suspicious of some of the people he's getting mixed up with, he accuses me of doubting everyone as an excuse for not being committed.'

'You surely can't think he'd listen to *me*. I'd sound like any other gringo who's always urging the morality of non-violent means on those his country keeps down by force.'

'I didn't mean just talk to him. If you could find out something about those he's working with...'

'Well...' doubtfully.

'I don't want you to do anything dangerous; but since you *do* seem to know some of them—you see, Kyle, I'm not like Papa. I'm proud of Juan for what he feels and what he's doing. I only want to be reassured that it's not some crack-brained scheme that's going to get them in trouble or that he's not being made use of by those less sincere than he is himself.'

'Naturally.'

'This is not like your country,' she continued. 'There, if you get out of line, you may find yourself doing a period in jail. Here...'

'I know, Ana.' I made a gesture with my forefinger of having my throat cut. 'But mind you, that's not why I hesitate. Or at least it isn't the only reason. I'm simply not at all certain that I can find out much. After all, if I *could* discover what they're up to, that in itself would be a pretty damning indictment of their security arrangements. You could almost say that if I could find out what they're doing, they'd better drop it.'

'I understand.'

But she looked so disappointed that I could not leave it there. 'Still,' organising a cheerful smile to show her, 'there are one or two leads I might follow up. I don't know if it'll do much to allay your fears; but...'

'You must promise me you won't take any chances,' she said quickly. 'It wouldn't help me to have to worry about you, too.'

Put like that, of course, my mind was made up for me—even if I should come to regret it later. It looked as though I would probably be making that trip to the coast with Horace Watson after all.

I paid our bill and we went outside to find the carriage waiting for us.

I assisted Ana to mount and to the grinning old man : 'Home, James, and don't spare the passengers.'

5

'Just for the Ride'

HORACE WATSON seemed pleased to see me when I went to his room early the next morning. He had been gloomily stowing a few things in a small suitcase; but at the sight of my own bag he smiled and even made a joke.

'I suppose it's being fat that does it,' he said. 'People automatically distrust a fat priest or a fat revolutionary.'

'And how wrong they are! It's chaps like me with a lean and hungry look you want to look out for—particularly if they haven't come by it honestly. I eat my damn head off.'

'While I hardly have any appetite at all,' he told me. 'Life's not fair, is it?'

'Not very.'

'Still,' he shrugged, 'that gives us something to work on. Glad you decided to come with me. What made you change your mind?'

'You know me—anything to do a friend a favour.'

'But I don't reckon I'm the friend.'

A boy brought in a tray with coffee and toast.

'It's all I ever have for breakfast,' Watson explained. 'If you want something more . . .'

'No, this is fine. My healthy appetite doesn't get up till much later in the day.'

When we went downstairs, the car Watson had hired for the drive to the coast was parked in front of the hotel. A porter was putting a sample case labelled 'Allied Chemi-

71

cals Inc.' in the boot; and the driver lounged against the wing smoking a brown cigarette.

'Hi, boss,' he said with a grin as we approached the car.

Watson must have employed him before because he said : 'I don't know why you call me boss. You never do anything I tell you to.'

'At your service, boss.' The man saluted and opened the rear door for us to get in.

'Now look, Miguel,' Watson told him, 'I don't have an appointment at Costaplana till late this afternoon. That means you can average twenty-five or thirty miles an hour and we'll make it easily.'

'Right, boss.'

We had hardly settled ourselves in the back seat when Miguel shot away from the hotel and with rapid changes in gear had us racing along the narrow road to the Pass at seventy.

'A land of extremes,' I muttered to myself, recalling last night's experience with the carriage as a pleasant distraction from the fear of imminent death which our present pace inspired.

Watson and I did not talk much at first. We were too busy hanging on to our respective straps and seeking the kind of inner composure which would be appropriate for meeting one's end.

He did say between clenched teeth during a sickening skid in the dust : 'It's always like this,' with a jerk of his head toward our driver. 'You wouldn't believe that Miguel, when he's not behind the wheel of an automobile, is an ordinary, decent human being who's kind to his wife and children and doesn't beat dogs.'

'Why do you hire him?' I asked with a trace of bitterness.

'I don't. He's assigned to me. That hiring business is part of my act as a commercial traveller.'

'You mean he's really in on the plot?'

'That's what they tell me. My personal view is that he's working for the Federales and has been commissioned to kill us all off.'

We roared over the pass and dropped down into the valley beyond. At one point I tapped Miguel on the shoulder to lodge a protest of my own, only to have him turn around without reducing speed and explain at length that I had nothing to worry about. I did not try that again!

Once we were out of the mountains and belting along the plain tilting down to the coast, I was introduced to a local form of Russian roulette. The road was only wide enough for one car, with soft sandy shoulders at the side. The idea of the game was that Miguel drove at top speed toward any approaching motorist, gambling that the other driver would turn off into the dust when he realised that we had no intention of giving way. The fun of the thing was that most of the cars coming in our direction were driven by people only slightly less convinced than Miguel that the other fellow always turned off in the end.

I could not bear to watch. I turned to Watson. 'There's one thing that puzzles me. I can't see how a lot of what's going on fits into any scheme for getting Manuel Ortiz out of prison.'

Miguel's driving must have reduced him to such a state of jitters that he was in no condition to observe his usual caution in speaking of these things.

'You might as well know,' he said fatalistically. 'We probably won't live long enough for it to make any difference, anyway. There's a government armoury at Melina, which is on the other side of that spur of mountains just north of San Pedro.'

'Where El Huero and the others have their headquarters?'

'That's right. The plan is that simultaneously with the release of Ortiz there'll be an attack on the armoury.'

'But that's crazy!'

'What's so crazy about it? After the attack, our people move back into the mountains with whatever arms and ammunition they've captured. They're safe enough there. Meanwhile Ortiz is out of jail and all over the country it'll be assumed that he's leading the rebellion. He has a tremendous following among the people, you know. There'll be risings in other places and men will begin to collect at various points in the Cordilleras.'

'And what'll the armed forces be doing?'

'Chasing themselves ragged trying to pin-point this little group or that as incidents occur in widely separated places. All hit-and-run tactics, you see—carefully co-ordinated to keep the national forces off balance. It can be done.'

'Oh sure,' sarcastically; 'and the United States will sit back and watch it all happening with the same impartial interest they take in the World Series.'

'Naturally not. As soon as it becomes obvious that the rebellion might be making some headway, our government will intervene. We have to expect that. But even so—well,' he shrugged, 'there's Cuba.'

'I still think it's crazy,' I told him.

'You're not a poor peon, are you?'

'Don't get me wrong. I'm not *against* a move to throw the Yankees out of *any* country down here. Hell, haven't I been doing everything I can think of to avoid them myself? I'm just not convinced that it can be done.'

'Convincing you isn't the problem.'

It was stifling in the car. We had to keep the windows closed because of the thick dust. Watson's face was shiny with sweat and his cheeks quivered with the jolting of our race along the pitted road.

I shook my head doubtfully and turned away from him. The trouble was that I had already leapt to so many conclusions about the man and then had to rub them out that his image had become completely smudged in my mind. Was I going to have to try to impose on that marked-out and scribbled-over figure the idea that he was some kind of hero of our times?

A lorry bore down on us and I faced Watson again in order not to have to watch the result of another of Miguel's gambles.

'I take it you're responsible for the arms being smuggled in for the attack on the armoury.'

'That's right. We're going to the coast to arrange for them to be taken back into the mountains till they're needed.'

'I don't suppose you want to say where they come from?'

'I don't.'

'And you claim that it's not just a job as far as you're concerned?'

He looked at me before answering; and then he turned his head away as he spoke. 'I don't like danger. I don't get any kick out of risking my life at all. Do you think I couldn't have landed some nice safe post back in the States that would've suited me better than this?' He reached inside his crumpled jacket and pulled out the revolver I had seen before. 'They don't really go together, do they? The gun and that hand? I ought to've been a store clerk or a cashier in a bank. I guess I've told myself a dozen times over these last few years that I was in the wrong racket and that as soon as the job I was on was finished I'd get out of it.'

'Why haven't you?'

'I guess there're things I hate more than being scared half to death.'

'I see.' Suddenly I knew why I was so reluctant to change my mind about Watson. I was not at all certain that there was anything *I* hated more than being frightened out of my wits. In fact, ever since this maniac Miguel had taken my life in his hands, I had been cursing myself for the romantic impulse which had led me to accompany Watson.

'Tell me about Juan Gabaldon,' I begged. 'How did he get involved?'

'He was active in the youth movement. He was one of those who was sentenced to several months in jail for organising the demonstration in the capital two years ago. And, of course, he's a friend of Ribera's.'

'Ribera?'

'Didn't El Huero mention him? He's one of the chief architects of the whole plan. Of course that's not his real name; but he's always been known as Ribera. The police have been hunting for him ever since the raid on the local government offices in Rosario—oh, six or seven years ago now. Practically every violent act committed anywhere in the country gets blamed on Ribera.'

'What do you think of young Gabaldon?'

'He's a fine kid; but too hot headed—too anxious to show he's as good a patriot as any peasant with nothing to lose.' Watson frowned. 'Of course you've got to realise that any of these men might be government spies for all I know.' He turned his small eyes on me. 'Just as you might be a spy from the North.'

'As *you* might be, for all I know.'

'That's true, from your point of view. I'm the only person in this entire business I don't *think* is a spy. But that doesn't help much. You see,' he said gloomily, 'I could still make some stupid mistake, like shooting my mouth off the other evening when I didn't realise you

were in the room; and the results would be just as dis-
astrous as if I *were* a spy.'

'It's a tough game,' I agreed. 'I don't want any part
of it myself.'

He tucked the revolver away. 'I really do think I'll give
it up after this one. This is the biggest thing I've ever had
a hand in. If this goes right, I believe I can retire.'

'And if it doesn't?'

'The question of retirement probably won't arise.'

We sped up over a sandy crest and had our first sight of
the blue Gulf.

'You see, boss,' Miguel turned around to say with a
triumphant grin, 'I bring you to the coast safe and sound.'

'We're not there yet,' Watson yelled pointing a stubby
finger at the road ahead.

Costaplana turned out to be a cluster of poor huts and
a few large stone buildings, from the midst of which a long
wooden pier ran out into the water. Several boats bobbed
along the length of the pier and on the curving beach
brown nets were drying on poles stuck into the sand.

One of the stone buildings was the town's only hotel,
and combined the functions of bar, restaurant and
general meeting place as well. While Miguel parked the
car, we went inside, causing a flutter of conversation
among those grouped around the bar. Foreigners from
the north were obviously something of a novelty in
Costaplana.

Watson asked the barman, who was also hotel
manager, porter, head waiter and possibly cook, if there
was a message for him. There was not.

'Have a drink,' I urged, noticing how worried he
looked. 'It'll damp down the dust in our throats.' And to
the barman I said in Spanish: 'Have one on us.' It was
not just generosity. I wanted to see if he was prepared
himself to swallow the brownish liquid he was serving.

77

We took our drinks over to a little table under the window. I raised my glass to salute the men who were staring at us as though we were some very odd form of marine life they might have dragged up in their nets.

'What do we do now?' I asked Watson.

'Wait. What else *can* we do? I thought there might be a message of some kind; but probably he'll get in touch with us later.' He glanced at the men who continued to look at us from time to time as they talked among themselves. 'He'll know we're here, anyway,' Watson added. 'I should think the whole town'll know soon.'

'I suspect that *is* the whole town,' jerking my head toward the group at the bar. 'Who is it we're waiting to hear from?'

'He's called Mora. That's all I know. He organised some fishermen to receive the stuff and hide it. We'll take delivery from him.'

'One more thing. What am I supposed to be? I mean, I feel that I ought to be playing a part of some kind.'

'You're doing fine as a tourist. Your Spanish is almost as bad as mine.'

'Thanks!' I finished my drink. 'That's not as bad as it looks. Do you want another?'

'I think we ought to take a couple of rooms and wait there. Our man may not want to contact us in such a public place.'

'Good. I wouldn't mind restoring to the nation that portion of her sacred soil I'm carrying around with me.'

It required a united linguistic effort for us to convince the cantinero, in his guise of hostelero, that we really wanted to stay there for the night. He was sure we were looking for a motel twenty miles up the coast that catered for the likes of us.

'It's our car,' I explained. 'There's something wrong with it. Keeps getting out of control.'

At last we succeeded in talking him into letting us have the keys to two rooms on the floor above.

I was pleased to find my room so bare. The fewer hiding places for scorpions, tarantulas or just cockroaches the better. 'Ride a cock roach' was a phrase that had several times leapt to my mind as a description of my somewhat ludicrous and entirely unintentional involvement in this whole Pancho Villa type affair.

I stripped to the waist and washed in a tin basin, put on a clean shirt and joined Watson in his room which was several doors down the corridor from my own.

He was not very good company. He kept looking at his watch and getting up to go out onto the balcony that ran along one side of the building.

'What you need,' I told him, 'is a good stiff shot of the wonder-drug, Metazone. Too bad it's only one of your props.'

It seemed to me a long time since we had eaten the sandwiches and fruit we had taken with us from the hotel. I offered to go downstairs and get us some supper.

'Go ahead,' Watson said. 'I'm not hungry.'

'You ought to eat all the same.'

'I think something's gone wrong. He ought to have been here before this.'

'Me, I like to do my worrying on a full stomach.'

I went down to the bar and persuaded the hostelero, in his guise of cocinero, to whip up something for us.

One of the regulars took over the bar in his absence; and I bought the crowd a round of drinks. Using the same bid for cheap popularity I had tried several times before, I lifted my glass and said 'Viva Castro.'

It had the effect of setting them all to arguing so violently among themselves that I was completely forgotten in the heat of the debate. I decided I was no more cut out to be a politician than a spy.

When I returned to Watson's room with two plates of omelets on a battered tin tray, he was standing on the balcony. I went and stood beside him.

The little town was blood red in the light which came out of the dusty west where the sun was in its death throes. Curving away to the south was a crescent shore of scarlet-tinted sand and the waves frothed into crimson bubbles as they broke along the beach with a muted roar.

'Funny thing,' Watson shook his head. 'My life has taken me to some beautiful places; but I was always so wrapped up in what I was doing I hardly noticed. I've met some interesting people too; but to me they were only men I had to fix up some deal with, men I wasn't sure whether I could really trust or not. Somehow I've always missed out on the excitement and comradeship of popular struggles. I've always been like, I don't know, like the guy who's only responsible for the props when they're staging a big show.'

'Well,' I told him, 'the best actor in the world would look pretty silly if he got to the high point of the play and reached out for the pistol which is going to make a hell of a bang waking up all the people in the back rows—and it wasn't there!'

'I guess so. But just once I'd like to have done the El Huero sort of thing.'

'Come inside and have something to eat.'

He returned to the room dispiritedly and picked at his omelet without making much headway in dispatching it.

'What about our driver?' I asked.

'Miguel makes his own arrangements. He'll be around when we want him.'

'*I* don't want him. I think I'll take one of the local coaches for the return trip.'

'That's how Miguel learned to drive as he does—on a local coach run.'

'Well,' philosophically, 'I suppose it's just a question of whether one of the cars whizzing around down here has got your name on it.'

Watson looked at his watch and frowned. He got up and began pacing around the room.

'Hey,' I said. 'Take it easy. We don't need to get upset because somebody in this timeless land fails to turn up when expected. It's punctuality that ought to make us suspect something's up.'

'You don't get it,' Watson stopped to explain. 'The more I think about it, the less reason I see for me to have been sent here at all. Getting the stuff up into the mountains could've been handled without me. Once the shipment arrived, my job was over.'

'Who did send you here?'

'I received my instructions in the usual way. But if I can't see any point in this trip, I'm bound to think the real reason wasn't given me.'

'Well,' even more philosophically when it was someone else's problem, 'we *are* here. We'll just have to wait and see what happens.'

He glanced at me irritably and continued his pacing.

I went downstairs and got some drink, thinking it might help him pass the time less nervously. But after an hour or so of trying unsuccessfully to distract him with idle talk, I yawned and stretched.

'I'm going to turn in. That ride took a lot out of me.'

He had not seemed to get much comfort from my presence; but he did not want me to leave either.

'There's another drink or so in the bottle,' he said.

I remained for another half hour; but by then I was practically asleep in my chair.

'That finishes the bottle *and* me.' I drained my glass and got up.

'I don't guess I'll be able to sleep a wink,' he complained.

'You ought to try,' I advised. 'If we don't hear anything in the morning let's go back to San Pedro and see if we can find out what this was all about.'

'I'd like to go back now,' he said.

'I don't much fancy a *night* drive with Miguel at the wheel. Of course, if we could get the keys from him and drive back ourselves . . .'

Watson was weighing the whole thing up, his face brightening briefly as he toyed with the idea of getting out of there at once. But then, features sagging, he said : 'I guess we ought to stay till tomorrow morning anyway.'

I returned to my room and stripped off my shirt. Before undressing any farther I went out to find the W.C. I worked my way along the corridor, trying various doors without finding the right one. There was another flight of stairs at that end of the building and I went down to the ground floor. The only convenience was evidently an outhouse I finally found at the back.

When I had climbed the stairs, I stopped where I was in the half light of one dim bulb. Two men were standing outside the door of my room.

I assumed they must have knocked while I was away; but for some reason I stayed there at the shadowy end of the hall. They turned away and walked toward Watson's room, paused a moment and then went quickly inside.

I cannot say what it was about those two men that had made me act like that. The instant I saw them waiting silently in front of the door of my room I had felt a shock of fear. Then, as soon as they disappeared, I ran quietly down the corridor, slipped into my room and fastened the bolt.

I stood there with my back to the door while my heart slugged heavily against my ribs. I could not remember hearing Watson lock his own door as I left, so it had been possible for those men to walk in on him without warning. Would they want to surprise him like that if they meant him no harm?

I knew I ought to go down there and see what was happening; but it took me a moment or so to turn and grasp the knob of the bolt.

I had an idea. Leaving my door locked I crossed the room and stepped out on the balcony. I crept along on tiptoe till I was opposite Watson's room and looked inside. There was no light and I could not see anyone at all.

Again it took a couple of moments for me to force myself to go in. 'Watson,' I called softly. There was no answer.

In the dark I bumped into a chair before I realised that Watson was sitting in it. 'Watson!' I whispered urgently, putting my palm on his shoulder. I touched a warm, sticky mess at the juncture of his neck and jerked my hand away. I sprang to the door and switched on the light.

Watson sat staring at the floor, head dropped forward over a jagged cut from ear to ear, a great gout of blood oozing down over his vest. Something rose in my throat and choked me—either vomit or the beginning of a yell.

Then I heard footsteps coming back along the corridor. They must have seen the light underneath the door. My hand was trembling so violently I could hardly slam the bolt home before I heard pressure being applied on the other side and heavy breathing.

I rushed out onto the balcony and back to my own room. I stood in the centre of the floor glancing about wildly and wondering what I was going to do. Why had I not looked for Watson's revolver while I was there? My breath came in painful gasps and my heart beat so hard I was afraid it would damage itself. I was still standing there in a complete funk when I saw the door forced against the bolt by someone pushing at it.

I grabbed up my shirt and jacket and ran out on the balcony. I climbed over the iron railing, let myself down till I was hanging by my fingers and dropped. It was not much of a fall. I found my clothes and ran off as fast I could, dodging down an alley and racing past a row of houses.

I kept on running. It was as if running was all my body ever wanted to do again and I would never be able to stop running. I ran along a narrow lane and came to the main street of the little town. I was still running when I reached the last few houses and I ploughed on over several low dunes filling my shoes with loose sand till I came to the hard-packed sand close to the water's edge. I jogged along the beach and only stopped when my lungs were pumping too painfully for me to continue.

I looked behind me, but I could not see anyone. Bent nearly double I sucked in the wet salt air and gradually got over my panic.

Would they be looking for me or was their work complete now that they had killed Watson? There was no point in taking any risks. I took off my shoes and waded through the foam to leave no footprints.

When I had gone some distance I saw a clump of wind-racked bushes growing between mounds of sand. I crossed the beach and pushed my way into this scrub growth where I flopped on my back utterly exhausted.

Poor Watson, I thought. He must have been expecting something like that. If only we had left as soon as he began to be suspicious.

And what was *I* going to do? I could not go to the police. Under the circumstances that would be ridiculous. 'You see, señor el guardia, we were minding our own business plotting the overthrow of your state when these

84

two villains . . .' I giggled in the last ebbing waves of the hysteria which had gripped me back there in the hotel. Even if I dared return to the town, I could hardly go about knocking on the doors of strangers and asking them to take me in.

Besides I did not want to be around when Watson was discovered. I could not answer the questions which were bound to be asked without betraying others. I did not even know how to find Miguel; and if I did, there was no way of being sure he might not have had a hand in Watson's assassination.

I was in a proper jam all right. I had better stay right where I was and perhaps I would think of something in the morning. If I ever saw it. I rose to my knees and poked my head up high enough to look back along the shore. I could not see anything but the breakers looking faintly luminous in the starlight.

I lay down again. I tried to listen for anyone coming along the beach; but my ears were full of the sound of the waves. I intended to stay awake till dawn; but bodily fatigue defeated me in the end. I slept and when I awoke my first thought was of Watson. Poor old fellow. He would never be able to do his El Huero act now.

But the thing that had been worrying me before I dropped off to sleep seemed perfectly simple. Of course I could not go back to Costaplana. There was only one course open to me—walk across country till I was some distance away, then hit the road leading inland and thumb a ride to San Pedro. Most of the traffic would be from farther along the coast and I would be unlikely to get picked up by anyone who knew anything about the murder.

With my jacket slung over my shoulder I set forth, walking west and keeping roughly parallel to the road. I spent the first part of my journey trying to decide if the

police would be able to trace me. I had left my small suitcase at the hotel but there was nothing in it but extra
socks and underwear, my pyjamas and shaving kit. None
of these things, as far as I could remember, had any dis-
tinguishing marks on them. And Watson and I had
never been asked to register.

Still, if they were really determined to find who had
been there with Watson, they would probably run me to
earth. I would just have to ask Barry Jones what I ought
to do—in their interests as well as my own. I wished to
hell I had never got mixed up in any of it; but thinking
back I could not recall any one point at which I had been
guilty of meddling in what was none of my business. The
whole affair had simply reached out and enmeshed me
through a series of what, discreetly, looked like the most
random accidents but taken all together was beginning
to have the grim feel of fate.

By ten o'clock it was already very hot and my eyes were
beginning to ache a bit from the blinding sunlight. As I
left the coast behind, the ground became stony and uneven, cactus and thorn bushes necessitated many irritating little detours. I could mark the course of the road off to
my right by the dust thrown up from infrequent cars.

An hour later I had joined the road and was trudging
along a few yards to one side. Two automobiles passed
churning up such clouds of dust that I had to put my
handkerchief over my nose to breathe. They disappeared
toward the distant blue line of the mountains with my
curses as thick in their wake as the dust.

By twelve I was extremely thirsty and trembling with
weariness. The dust had caked on me while there was still
moisture enough in my body for perspiration and now it
had dried so that I looked like a mummy stumbling along
beside the highway. In lucid moments I had to admit that

nothing would have prevailed on *me* to stop for such a creature.

At last when I had just about decided that I would show them all by going off and dying quietly under a large cactus, a car did slow down and stop.

I ran forward joyfully and then pulled up when I saw who was driving. It was Miguel.

I stood there eyeing him distrustfully.

'I know what happened,' he told me. 'I heard about it this morning from the people I was staying with. I looked for you; but no one knew where you were. I am very glad to see you, señor.'

'I don't know whether I'm glad to see you or not.'

'But we must get back to San Pedro quickly and explain what's happened to Señor Watson.'

I shrugged. It might be quicker than going off and dying under my cactus. 'Have you any water?' I asked.

'No; but there's a place about half an hour from here where you can get a drink.'

A half hour of *his* driving meant that it must be some forty miles away! I got in the front beside him and we shot off toward the mountains.

Perhaps it was my recent experiences which had altered my perspective. Miguel's duels with death did not seem so frightening any more. Indeed, I slept most of the way back.

6

'We Believe You Can Swing It'

I HAD Miguel drop me at the hotel. I wondered what the other guests were making of me—a man who was usually out all night and then either arrived in a car that ought to be in the Smithsonian Institute or staggered in looking like a fugitive from the Egyptian room at the Metropolitan Museum. They must think I had tapped a source of perverted pleasures in this little town the guide books were discreetly silent about. I also wondered if I could arrange some sort of discount for the times my bed remained unslept in.

After a bath, two baths in fact since the first merely softened up my outer rind, I felt better. But I did not want to hang around the hotel. When I was not actively doing something, I was haunted by the image of that figure slumped in a chair, head dropped forward in the red slime on his chest.

I shook my head to dislodge the memory and went downstairs. Outside, the old man in the victoria looked at me hopefully; but I signalled for a taxi and directed the driver to drop me within a short distance of that house I had been taken to after the bull fight.

After a bit of searching through the meaner quarter, I found the place and knocked on the door.

It was opened by Pérez who immediately embraced me and yelled for Rosa.

'He's come,' he told her when she appeared in the doorway. 'We'll have a big dinner in honour of our distinguished guest who makes us laugh.'

'Hey!' I said. 'I haven't come here to invite myself to dinner. It's important for me to see El Huero. Can it be arranged?'

'For you it can be arranged, I think. And while we are waiting, Rosa will prepare for us a fine meal.'

He made me sit down; and with a flourish like a magician's he produced from his pocket a large Havana cigar. 'I have been saving it for you,' he beamed. 'Viva Castro, eh, señor?'

'Viva Castro!' accepting the gift.

'By the time you have smoked it, I'll be back. Then,' rubbing his hands, 'we will dine together.'

'But what about my seeing El Huero?'

'Leave it to Pérez,' he said with a wink.

I sat there as evening came on, puffing the cigar appreciatively and listening to the pleasant domestic clatter which came from the kitchen. I remembered sleeping in this very room with Watson standing—or rather, sprawling guard over me. 'Revolutions make strange bedfellows,' I reflected a little sadly—'and for some, indeed for many, the sleep is permanent.'

When Pérez returned, Juan Gabaldon was with him. We shook hands formally and Juan sat down opposite me while Pérez went into the back of the house to get something for us to drink.

'What have you been up to now?' he asked me.

'I'd prefer to talk to Barry Jones.'

'You probably will. I'm waiting to hear if and when and where he can see you.'

'Good.'

Juan frowned. 'It's very strange. You insist that it's only an accident that you ever got involved with us; and yet it goes on happening, doesn't it?'

'What precisely are you referring to?' I asked cautiously.

'Your trip to the coast with Watson of course.'

'You know about that.'

'We knew within an hour or so of your leaving the hotel together.'

'And also what happened when we got there?'

'All I know is that you came back and Watson didn't. Others may know more; but that's not the point. If you never wanted to get mixed up in our affairs, why did you go with Watson in the first place?'

'Partly because he asked me to. He had this idea, and how right he was! that there was something fishy about the trip. But the main reason I went with him was you.'

'Me!'

'Yes. You see your sister is worried about you. She asked me to try to find out something about the people you're working with.'

'Oh my God!' he exclaimed. He got up and walked about the room. He turned on me suddenly. 'But I told you she was hopeless when it came to politics. What right has she to set some idiot from the north to spy on me?'

'Now just a minute. I resent that remark. I may be from the north and I'm certainly an idiot; but I can't have you casting aspersions on your sister's genuine concern for you.'

'If you only knew how hard I've tried to escape from my family background!'

'I appreciate that, Juan. I realise that a serious revolutionary *has* no family but his comrades in struggle. Ana doesn't want to hold you back. She just wants to be reassured that those you're working with now are worth your loyalty.'

'And she believes that someone like you can judge them!'

'She may. I don't. Oh I admit I had no right to let her think I could ease her mind about you. I tried to tell her that; but I probably didn't try as hard as I should have.'

'But don't you see what sort of position it'll put me in when you say that you went with Watson because of me?'

'What makes you think I'd say such a thing? As far as anyone else is concerned, I went with Watson because he asked me to. That's all there is to it.'

He stood there looking down at me. 'Thanks,' he said at last. Then: 'I'm sorry. I've been doing you an injustice.'

'Maybe not,' I told him. 'There's no reason why you should trust me. I don't particularly want you to, Juan. I just want you, for Ana's sake, to be a bit cautious with others as well.'

'What's Ana to you?' And when I hesitated, 'Of course,' he said, 'that question may seem odd since I've told you that I've repudiated my family. Still, I'm very fond of Ana.'

'So am I. Nothing more. She's simply a very lovely young woman I'd prefer to think of as happy. You mean a lot to her you know.'

'I wish the things I believe in meant as much.'

'Perhaps they do. People express these things in different ways.'

'There are times when only one form of expression is valid.'

'That's true; but even in a revolutionary struggle people have different rôles to play. You'll be surprised at some of the people who'll turn out to be on your side after all.'

'And some who'll prove to have been against us all along.'

'That too.'

91

Juan sat down again. He offered me a cigarette and, looking at me searchingly : 'Tell me,' he asked. 'I believe you're sympathetic to our cause. Does that mean you go all the way with us?'

'What would be the point of my trying to answer that? I could say I do and not mean it or I could mean it and find that in the event I wasn't *capable* of going all the way. In certain situations our judgements about other individuals, even about ourselves, have to be more pro-visional than at other times. All that counts is what those individuals actually do under stress.'

'We have to trust our leaders if the movement is to succeed,' Juan insisted.

'Not uncritically.'

'Not uncritically,' he agreed. 'Ultimately one trusts the people themselves. It's the response of the people which is the test of leadership.'

That was true enough in the long run I supposed; but it did not help much with the problem of deciding at any given moment in whom to put one's faith. I wondered if my confidence in Barry Jones was simply a matter of having known about him over such a long period or whether it might not involve some prejudice in favour of a fellow Anglo-Saxon. 'Anyway,' I said to Juan, 'if you see Ana, I hope you'll reassure her on the score of looking out for yourself.'

'I'll do better than that,' he smiled. 'I'll tell her I'm looking out for you as well.'

Pérez brought some earthenware mugs and a couple of bottles of beer. We sat there drinking and chatting for a half hour or so.

I looked at my watch. 'I don't want to give the im-pression that I'm not enjoying myself; but what about my wanting to see El Huero?'

'That's been taken care of,' Juan told me. 'He may be coming here.'

'Yes,' Pérez nodded. 'Rosa is cooking more food in case he comes. He won't be alone.'

'Isn't it dangerous for him to be seen in town?'

Juan shrugged. 'Everything is dangerous for a man like El Huero. But he won't be arriving till after dark.'

And not long after night had fallen there was a disturbance among the chickens at the back of the house. The two Mexicans I had seen outside the hut where I had met Jones came in from the kitchen. One of them had a bandoleer slung across his shoulder and carried a carbine cradled in his arm. He nodded to Juan and Pérez and went out through the curtain to stand in the shadows by the front door. The other with a pistol in a holster at his hip took up his post in an angle of the room and lit a small cigar.

Only when these men were in position did El Huero enter the room. He too had a pistol hanging from a cartridge belt. He smiled at us, his teeth looking very white against his sun-darkened face, and moving the holster out of the way he sat down.

Juan jerked his head toward me. 'He said it was important.'

El Huero nodded. 'You did right, Juan. If our friend, Kyle, hadn't sought me out I'd have been looking for him.'

Pérez got up. 'I'll see how Rosa is getting on with the meal. You'll have something with us, jefe?'

'Thank you, Pérez.' He turned to me and the smile disappeared. 'Why did you go to Costaplana with Watson?'

'Because he asked me to.'

'That was foolish.'

'For him to ask me?'

93

'For you to go with him.'

'I don't think so. Watson was worried—with every justification! It seemed little enough for me to do. No one had told me *not* to go.'

He shook his head disapprovingly. 'No one had told you not to talk about what you now know in the bar of the Hotel *Buena Vista*. Some things one leaves to common sense.'

'Well,' bridling a little, 'I'm damned glad I did go. I didn't do anything to prevent what happened to Watson; but if I was any company for him in the last hours he spent here...'

El Huero held up his hand to stop me. 'I take it you liked Watson.'

'I liked the *idea* of Watson. He wasn't particularly likeable and certainly didn't appear in the least heroic; but all the same he died in the struggle to set this country free.'

'Granted. In his own way Watson *was* a hero. He won't be forgotten.' Jones lit a cigarette. 'Will you tell me what happened?'

I hesitated a moment, studying that square strong face. 'You've already heard about it from Miguel.'

'I *have* talked with Miguel. But I want to hear it from you, Kyle. You were right there.'

'There's not much to tell. We went to that hotel near the beach and waited for a man, I think Watson said his name was Mora. He never came. About ten o'clock I went to my own room. While I was out of it for a few minutes, two men came along. They killed Watson and I got the hell out of there. That's all there was to it.'

'Did you see them clearly, those two men? Would you recognise them if you saw them again?'

'No. They were at the other end of the corridor and the

94

only light was very dim. Would they have been working for the government?'

'Who knows,' Jones said. 'It's possible. Or they may have been paying off some old score out of Watson's past. A man makes enemies in a game like his.'

'If you've finished, Barry, I'd like to ask a few questions myself. When I talked with you, why didn't you tell me what this was all about? You let me think you were only involved in a scheme to get Ortiz out of prison. You didn't mention the guns or the raid on the arsenal or any of the rest of it, did you?'

'No, I didn't.'

'Why not? You said a lot at the time about the need to trust people and yet it's quite obvious that you didn't trust me at all.'

'That's one way of looking at it,' he said with a grin. 'But there's another way. We didn't want you to know more than was good for you.'

'It wasn't very good for me to get mixed up with Watson when I hadn't the most remote idea of what he was really doing.'

'You mean you wouldn't have gone with him if you'd known there was any real danger? I thought it was what had actually happened that made you glad you did go.'

'Maybe so; but you should've given my natural cowardice a chance to have its say in the matter.'

He looked me up and down appraisingly. 'That's just it. I don't believe you *are* a coward. Far from it.'

'You should've seen me high-tailing it down the beach,' I retorted—pleased in spite of myself.

'As for our trusting you,' Jones went on—'I've been talking about you to Ribera. But of course you probably haven't heard of Ribera.'

'I've heard of him.'

'Well, Ribera agrees that you're just the person to carry

out a special job for us. We've worked out a scheme for getting Manuel Ortiz out of prison. We need someone who can visit Ortiz and explain the plan to him. We believe you can swing it, Kyle.'

'I suppose I could try.'

'You see, we had you sort of ear-marked for that side of the operation, so there didn't seem to be any point in filling you in on what would be happening here. The less you knew about the attack on the arsenal the better it'd be for you if something went wrong and you were arrested. I don't see how you *could* get arrested; but it's just as well to be on the safe side. We don't want to expose you any more than is absolutely necessary.'

I nodded shrewdly. 'Yes, that figures.'

Jones reached in his pocket and pulled out a folded sheet of paper. 'It's all written down—the details for springing Ortiz. Memorise it, Kyle, and then burn it. Right?'

'Right.'

'You've got ten days to go to the capital and see if you can arrange an interview with Ortiz. The cultural attaché at the U.S. Embassy can help. So can the vice-president of the University. Think you can manage it?'

'I can try,' I said again.

'You can leave San Pedro the day after tomorrow by bus. The trip takes about four hours. And, Kyle . . . ?'

'Yes?'

'During tomorrow see if you can stay out of trouble, will you? Try not to get mixed up in any riots in the Mercado Central. If bandits attempt to rob the local bank, let the police handle it. Try, just for one day, to mind your own business and not get involved in other people's problems.'

'Now look, Barry . . .'

'I know. It's never your fault. These things get thrust

upon you. But this is a serious business and we need your help. So, for a little while, till we can get Ortiz out of jail, concentrate on the matter in hand.'

'You make me sound like a goddamned fool,' I protested.

'Not at all. But you must admit that you seem to be disaster prone. We don't want our whole scheme blowing up in our faces because you happened to blunder in on it, do we?'

'You wait and see how I handle the business of getting your message to Ortiz,' I told him with determination.

'Good man.' And turning to Juan : 'Perhaps you could spend tomorrow with him—just to keep perfect strangers from imposing on his good nature and enlisting his aid in wild ventures.'

'I think I know a better way of keeping him out of mischief,' Juan said with a wink.

'Go ahead,' I said. 'Make as much fun of me as you like. But have you considered the implications for your own security arrangements if a silly ass like myself *can* blunder into what's supposed to be a serious revolutionary attempt?'

'Ah,' Juan smiled. 'He's got something there, hasn't he?'

Pérez brought in a table and put it in the centre of the room. Rosa followed him with dishes of food from which we helped ourselves.

Barry Jones ate quickly and got up to go. He thanked Rosa and shook my hand.

'I hope it goes all right, Kyle. Kidding aside, I think you'll pull it off for us. With any luck, Ortiz will be free by the time you leave the capital. When you come back here, Pérez will tell you how to get in touch with me. Ribera will probably want to see you as well, and we can discuss the question of what happens next. You may be able to do a lot for us once you're back in the States.'

'*If* I go back.'

'We'll talk about it later.'

Barry Jones turned to go out the back way, preceded by the man who had stood in an angle of the room eating from a plate Pérez had handed him. The man at the front of the house did not appear again.

It was only when they had gone that I realised I had not put the main question I had wanted to ask. 'What *had* been the purpose in sending Watson to Costaplana?' As before, I had been too much under El Huero's spell to bring up the points I had meant to raise with him.

It was not altogether surprising. That solid figure giving the impression of great physical power under complete control, that square brown face beneath the shock of blond hair with its look of frankness and confidence all added up to someone naturally commanding respect and admiration. When he had come into the room with his bodyguard, one's immediate feeling was that life did sometimes manage to single out for an important rôle a person who looked the part in every way.

We had coffee and chatted for a while. Then, after a somewhat effusive parting from Pérez and Rosa, Juan and I walked back through the town.

'Where are you living now?' I asked him—'if that's not indiscreet.'

'Most of the time I camp with the others,' gesturing toward the black shape of the mountains. 'When I have to come to town, I stay at the house of a friend who's working with us.'

'Don't you think your father would sympathise with what you're doing if you explained it to him?—in general terms of course.'

Juan shook his head. 'I've tried. You see, Kyle, he regards someone like Ribera as simply a bandit taking advantage of the people's misery to set himself up as a leader. My father still thinks it's merely a question of replacing certain corrupt figures in the government with men of integrity, like himself. How could he believe otherwise? In a sense he works for the present ruling class. He's their man. He may be critical in respect to specific acts of injustice like the imprisonment of Tio Manuel; but he's not prepared to see the whole filthy lot swept away.'

'All the same,' I said, 'I don't see why it wouldn't be possible for you two to be friendly and just agree to differ over politics.'

Again he shook his head. 'That kind of liberalism may work in the States where internal change isn't even an issue. Not here. Here there are only two sides. Those who passionately want a revolution to complete the struggle for independence which began years ago, and those who'll stop at nothing to prevent it. There *is* no middle ground. The line runs through this whole country and it can split families apart as easily as states.'

'I suppose you're right.'

'When we're really free, many who failed to support us in the struggle can be won over. But any compromise now would be fatal to our cause.'

'It seems rather sad though.'

'Only if you forget all the thousands of families that are continuously being split apart by poverty and oppression.' Juan stopped and held out his hand. 'I must leave you here.'

'Goodnight.'

'If I don't see you again before you go to the capital— good luck!'

'I thought you were supposed to look out for me tomorrow—to keep me out of trouble.'

'We'll see,' he laughed.

The next morning I got up early and had a quick breakfast with every intention of completing an article for the *Review* during the course of the day. If I did not get something off to the printers soon, they would think I had given up the idea of keeping the journal going at all. A piece on the analogy between artistic innovation and social revolution ought to fill up quite a few pages if I let myself go on it.

By eleven o'clock, when it was time for me to break off for coffee, there was nothing to break off *from*. Apart from the title neatly printed at the top of the page not a word had been written. Perhaps writing literary articles for my *Review* had merely been a reflex of the frustrated life I led in the States; and now that I was leading a different sort of life, such a response was no longer appropriate.

That itself, I decided, might make an interesting article —'the disappearance of the urge to write.' I tore up the first page and printed the new title at the top of a fresh sheet. But once I had written it down, I realised that it contained a paradox which proved to be absolutely inhibiting. After lunch I could return to the earlier theme.

But while I was sipping my coffee and working out a few parallels between the overturning of society and the upsetting of literary canons, Ana Gabaldon came into the dining room and approached my table.

She was wearing riding breeches which, clotheswise, are most women's worst enemies, but were firmly and faithfully on her side. A white silk blouse open at the neck completed her wardrobe.

I stood up and beckoned to a waiter to bring another cup.

'This is a very pleasant surprise,' I said.

'I was told that I was deputed to keep you out of trouble today.'

I glanced surreptitiously at that rather revealing blouse. 'You're kidding!'

'No, I'm perfectly serious,' without batting an eye. 'Juan met me in town this morning and insisted that I look after you.'

'Well, it's an idea,' I said dubiously. 'I'm just trying to recall whether I've ever been in any trouble which wasn't the direct result of women.'

'There are women and women,' she told me with a smile.

'There's trouble and trouble, too. I've heard it said of youth in the States that drink and dope and sex at least keep them out of mischief—meaning that it distracts them from any dangerous criticism of their own society.'

'It's not the most flattering comparison of my charms I've ever heard.'

'I was thinking of their effect rather than their quality. One look at you in that outfit and I'm high as a kite. Was it your idea to ride herd on me for the rest of the day?'

'We're both going riding. I've brought a horse for you.'

'What ever happened to the shy young ladies wearing mantillas and simpering behind grills who weren't allowed out of the house without a duenna?'

'Juan's not the only member of the family who's rebellious. Do you want to change into something else?'

'This is all right for me—if the horse doesn't object.'

Outside the hotel, at a tie rack I had never noticed before, were tethered the two horses. Looped over one of the saddle horns was a large sombrero.

'For me?'

'Yes. You probably aren't used to so much sun.'

'I ought to be. I got enough of it on my trip to the coast.'

'Tell me about it.'

'There's nothing much to tell,' I said evasively. I assisted her to mount, who needed no help, and then managed to get myself up, who possibly did. 'Putting me in hospital for a couple of days would certainly keep me out of mischief.'

'Pedro's well past his first youth. He won't give you any trouble.'

'Good. We can practise together growing old gracefully.' I donned my hat. 'How do I look?'

'Like an American tourist.'

'Thanks.'

She led the way across the road and down the slope to the little valley where a rivulet of spring water gurgled among the rocks. There were trees along the course and we rode leisurely through the dappled afternoon, splashing from time to time through the shallow stream. It was very pleasant renewing my acquaintance with the creak of leather and the smell of horse sweat.

Once as we rode abreast she said, 'Thank you for talking to Juan. He was almost civil to me in the market this morning.'

'Those who're hopeless at families of their own are probably good at other people's.'

'Do you think you'll ever try again, Kyle?'

'I doubt it. I can't imagine ever disliking a woman so much.'

'It must've been their fault. I should think you'd be easy to live with.'

'Well I'm not. I can hardly live with me myself.'

'That's your old trick of warning people off, isn't it?'

'Here! You're not suggesting it'd be necessary where you're concerned, are you, Ana?'

'Juan said you were going away for a while.' She ignored my question.

'That's true.'

'Will you be coming back to San Pedro?'

'I suppose so.'

'I'm glad.'

'Now look here, Ana. I don't want to jump to conclusions or anything like that; but I'd rather make a fool of myself than let there be any misunderstanding. You're probably better at horses. Have you had a good look at my teeth? I'm old enough to be your father.'

'You're old enough, I suppose; but, in spite of the impression you try to give, you're not detached enough. I think we may have to settle for some other relationship.'

'I don't mind standing in as uncle till such time as we can restore Tio Manuel to you.'

She shook her head. 'You'll have to let me work this out my own way.'

She turned off into a little glade in a bight of the stream and dismounted. 'We can rest here for a bit.'

'I'm not tired.'

'Pedro might be.'

I got down and loosened the girth.

'You know more about horses than you pretend. I'm learning not to believe anything you say about yourself.'

'It's a trick I picked up a long time ago, Ana. If you make yourself out worse than people think you are, they may not find out that you're even worse than that.'

'I make up my own mind about people.'

'Go ahead,' I shrugged. 'But don't say I haven't warned you.'

'Since you're old enough to be my father, Kyle, you ought to've learned something *he's* learned—that it's useless to oppose me when it comes to something I want.'

'I'll just have to see that you never want anything I think it'd be bad for you to have, won't I?'

7

'Madrugada Roja'

I GOT out of bed the next morning feeling stiff and sore
—not the best condition in which to face the prospect
of a four-hour ride on the hard seat of a bus.

After breakfast I arranged at the reception desk to dis-
continue my room for a week or so. I would write from
the capital when I expected to take up residence again.

'Shall we forward your mail, señor?'

'Any letters from the States you can put in chronologic-
al order according to the post marks and burn.'

Coaches for the capital left from a garage near the
Central Market. I arrived well before eleven with my one
suitcase—to be certain of a seat near the front, next to a
window.

It was a fairly safe assumption that I would not be
sharing a journey by such means with any tourists from
the North; but I did catch myself once, as the coach filled
up with passengers, looking around half expecting to see
Watson amongst them. It was strange. I had never intended meeting the man, had consistently avoided him
after a first chance encounter; and now I would never
forget him as long as I lived.

People were admitted long after every available seat
was taken; but it was pointed out to me that many
would be getting off at places only ten or twenty miles
away from San Pedro. I hoped that the family engulfing
me was one of these.

Most of the trip over the ridge of the Cordilleras and

down through the jungle-clad hills I sat staring out of
the window at a scene in which roads and villages and all
the works of man seemed irrelevantly adventitious. It was
not a landscape admitting of compromises, I thought in
recalling something Juan had said to me about his rela-
tions with his father.

What though, I wondered, was *I* doing in such circumstances, involved with such people as these recent companions of mine? I had always regarded myself as a very
shifty customer—not actually dishonest but very skilful
in evading any responsibilities the views I held might have
implied. I had always haunted the fringes of progressive
movements, had signed innumerable petitions, attended
countless meetings; but somehow, when it came to the
crunch, and a stand fraught with consequences had to be
taken, Kyle Brandeis was never there. How, then, had I
got mixed up with something like this? Did it mean that I
had really been a frustrated revolutionary all those years
and at last I was being presented with an opportunity to
express this thwarted impulse. Or was it simply that I
was yet to arrive at a stage where the going got rough
and I would do my usual vanishing act?

Just why had I gone along with them as far as I already
had? Did I really believe in what they were doing and,
if so, did I think they had a chance of pulling it off? Or
had I merely fallen under El Huero's influence? Jones
was a natural leader. I was just as naturally a born fol-
lower. There might not be more to it than that. When he
assumed unquestioningly that I would be only too willing
to perform any task he set me, who was I to raise objec-
tions?—at least as long as it did not cost me anything.

But *was* it going to cost me nothing? As El Huero himself had pointed out, this was a serious business. The
results for anyone involved in it could be grave indeed.
I knew I ought to be considering much more carefully

what I might be letting myself in for instead of simply drifting into it haphazardly. The trouble was that I could not really take myself seriously and it was difficult therefore to imagine the authorities taking me seriously either. Indeed, that might be El Huero's real reason for making use of me.

We stopped for lunch at a small town dwarfed by high trees and then after skirting a shallow body of water dotted with islands reached the outskirts of the capital in the early afternoon.

Juan had told me of a small clean cheap hotel not too inconveniently situated. The cheapness was essential. Conspiratorial activities did not seem to be any more financially rewarding as a profession than running small literary reviews.

The next morning I left the hotel and walked about the streets of town, partly to begin establishing myself as an ordinary tourist and partly because I have always *enjoyed* sight-seeing. That was what made my disguise so perfect. An ordinary tourist at heart pretending to be an ordinary tourist. One could hardly beat that for guile.

In the early afternoon I made my way to the United States Embassy and asked to see Arthur Howarth who, I had learned, was the cultural attaché. He could see me in half an hour, and I wandered about the foyer putting on my act of an ordinary tourist waiting to see a cultural attaché. I did it so successfully that thirty minutes later I was ushered into his office.

Howarth was a largish man in a crumpled linen suit who half rose from his chair at my entrance and waved me into the chair in front of his desk. He put his elbows on the desk top, rested his chin in his hands and stared at me rather intensely, eyebrows raised almost to the line of his crew-cut hair.

I stared back at him a few moments and then asked:

'Are you the Howarth who used to run the writers' workshop at Berkeley?'

'That's right.'

'And published a volume of verse called *The Angry Voice*?'

'Yes I did. Are you the Brandeis from England who edits the *Western Review*?'

'That's me. We ran some of your poems in one of our issues—oh about four years ago now.'

'I know. I remember there were several typographical errors in them.'

'Well it's a bit late to . . .'

'That's all right,' he said magnanimously. 'I wouldn't expect a magazine in the East, even if it is misleadingly called the *Western Review*, to cope with a literary revolution like the one we staged in California.'

'We're a pretty reactionary lot,' I admitted—'tricky too. What came after *The Angry Voice*?'

'Nothing. I did rather well out of that little volume and—to tell you the truth, once I'd made a bit of money and got in on the government service racket, I found I wasn't angry any more.'

'Washington's gain is literature's loss,' I said philosophically.

'It wasn't only that,' rubbing one hand over his cropped hair which struck an incongruous note with his loose bohemian figure. 'The powerful sex-imagery which made those poems such a wow came from the frustrations of a young man who couldn't afford women. Now,' he said lugubriously, 'I can afford them.'

'It's a problem,' I sympathised. 'One only seems to be able to write about them behind their backs, as it were.'

He visibly pulled himself together to cope with the functions of his post. 'What is it you want, Brandeis?'

'Well, I found myself here in the capital. I knew you

were in the Embassy here. I thought I'd interview you for
my review—"Epilogue to a Revolution", sort of thing.
That is, if you don't mind talking about yourself.'

He did not mind.

An hour or so later he paused for breath and then observed: 'You haven't been taking any of it down.'

'Photographic memory,' I explained. 'Thank you very
much for this interesting material.'

'Glad to be able to help.'

'There was just one other thing I wanted to ask you
about. My good friend at the University, Antonio
Zamora y Cadiz . . .'

'Delightful man!'

'Isn't he! Well, he hoped that while I was in town I
might be able to arrange an interview with Manuel
Ortiz.'

Howarth frowned. 'Difficult.'

'I realise that. But as you probably know, certain pink-
ish professors back home are making rather a lot of the
fact that Ortiz is a political martyr. It wouldn't hurt to
let the world know that, even if he has to be restrained in
the interests of the state, he isn't suffering unduly.'

'I suppose I could mention it to the first secretary.'

'My only concern of course is to discuss his poetry; but
incidentally, in setting the scene of the interview, I could
allay the disquiet felt about the conditions in which he's
held.'

'I'll certainly raise the matter,' Howarth promised. 'I
don't know what's got into academic people back home—
all this criticism of government policies they don't know
anything about.'

'Shocking!' I nodded. 'In Joe McCarthy's day teachers
stuck to their subjects and kids had some chance of getting
a good formal education; but now . . .'

'Now they spend all their time marching up and down

protesting about things they don't understand.'

'Of course they may be *healthier* than our generation.'

'Health isn't all that important,' he said. 'I sacrificed mine in Frisco dives and I've never regretted it.'

I left the address of my hotel with him so that he could get in touch with me.

The next morning I went to the University to keep an appointment I had made with Zamora y Cadiz. He was a wheel in the arts faculty and I had once corresponded with him about my article on Ortiz.

I arrived early and had time to wander about the campus looking at the modern buildings and splendid murals. This was fine revolutionary art, just as the writings of Ortiz were great revolutionary poetry. In this part of Central America, apparently, the artists were way out in front when it came to the transformation of society. The rest of the country was going to have to struggle like hell to catch up. Perhaps the historian of such a movement ought logically to be a critic of the arts like myself.

El Professor Zamora y Cadiz received me in a pleasant room at the disposal of senior members of the arts faculty. There was coffee and some delicious little cakes.

'It's very kind of you to see me,' I told him. 'I want to devote an issue of my review, perhaps several issues, to an appreciation of the best known writers in Latin America today. Remembering the assistance you gave me once before, I realised that no one could provide me with better guidance in this field than yourself.'

'I shall be glad to give you whatever help I can.'

'It's also a matter of personal satisfaction,' I added, 'to make the acquaintance of one whose articles in the *Nuevo Mundo* are well known to me.'

'You're too kind,' he acknowledged graciously.

'And incidentally,' hazarding a shot in the dark, 'Rafael

Gabaldon, whom I met during a short stay in San Pedro, asked me to convey his best regards.'

'Yes. We used to know each other well; but he comes to the capital all too seldom these days.' He got up and went over to a cupboard from which he took several periodicals. 'You'll find some worthwhile background material in these. How long do you intend remaining in the capital, Señor Brandeis?'

'A week to ten days.'

'Then it should be possible to arrange a small reception at which you could meet some of the younger writers.'

'That would be splendid.'

He talked for a while about some of these authors who had recently appeared on the literary scene; and then I explained that I must not take up any more of his time.

'There is one more little matter,' I told him as I prepared to leave. 'My friends at the American Embassy are very eager for me to see Manuel Ortiz while I'm here. They think it would be a good thing if his admirers in the States heard something about his present circumstances to counter the rumours which have gained a certain currency in academic circles there.'

'Difficult,' the professor pronounced.

'If you knew anyone in the government . . .'

'I'll have a word with the Minister of Culture. You'd be the right person to see Ortiz if it *could* be arranged, since you were instrumental in getting translations of his poems brought out in the United States.'

'A very great poet,' I said. 'It's a shame he couldn't have been inspired by less inflammatory subjects.'

'It isn't so much that he writes poems about revolution,' Zamora y Cadiz told me. 'He gets involved in actual revolutionary attempts. Ortiz' tragedy is that he's never been able to distinguish between literature and life. He has an unfortunate tendency to get the two hopelessly confused.

Still, I'll see what I can do about an interview while you're here.'

I left him the address of my hotel and went out into hot bright sunshine which dramatised the modern architecture of the University buildings, underscoring salient features with dark shadows and picking out in strokes of fire the brilliant frescoes.

While I was having lunch, another idea occurred to me. I remembered the name of the publishers with whom the North American edition of Ortiz' works had been arranged. They had an office just off the Calle Rivera; and I called in that afternoon. _Cop. 2_

I explained that a second printing was being considered and that a new preface was wanted which I would like to discuss with the poet himself.

The prospect of the dollars to be earned by another run made the man in charge of foreign rights listen with respect to my request.

I left their offices with the feeling that I had planted enough seedlings to get on with some serious sight-seeing while waiting for them to cross-fertilise each other.

It did not take long. Two days later an official-looking brown envelope was in my box when I came down to breakfast. I was informed that if I presented myself at the Federal Prison the following day, I would be permitted an interview with Manuel Ortiz.

In the general euphoria created by this evidence of the success of my scheming, I bought a picture postcard of the Museo Nacional and sent it to Ana.

I wandered happily about the city thinking of myself as something no well-organised subversive movement should be without. But then it stood to reason that the effortless guile, the endless subterfuges, the capacity to lie with a straight face, which anyone with a couple of wives like mine would have to master in the interest of survival,

ought to have some general application in the kind of
world we lived in. As El Huero had pointed out, this was
a serious business and the penalties for a false step could
be severe; but hell! when it came to torture, viciousness
and involuntary incarceration I had come up by way of a
pretty tough school myself. I bought two more picture
postcards of the Museo Nacional and sent them to those
women without whose attentions I would have been so
little fitted for the work in hand.

When the taxi dropped me outside the walls of the
prison the next afternoon, the grey, solid-looking fortress
had a sobering effect on me. There was something about
the wave of the driver when I had tipped him that suggested a final farewell to someone who is not likely to be
seen around for a long time.

Nothing, however, could have been more courteous
than my treatment by the prison officials once I had presented my letter at the main gate.

I learned from the guide who conducted me across the
courtyard and through the maze of corridors beyond, that
political prisoners were kept in a separate wing. We
climbed a metal stairway and walked along a high bridge
which communicated with the top floor of a building detached from the rest of the prison.

Half way down a dim hall we were met by a man whom
I took, from the magnificence of his uniform, to be a very
senior warden—if not the governor himself.

'Señor Brandeis,' he greeted me, holding out his hand,
'you do our establishment great honour by your visit to
one of our . . .' he smiled—'guests.'

'It is I, señor, who am honoured by this permission to
call on a friend in your care.'

He bowed slightly. 'We wish you to enjoy the greatest
possible freedom in your interview; but you will appreci-

ate that there are certain rules we are not in a position to waive.'

'Of course,' I nodded. 'We're all to some extent prisoners of whatever system we live under, aren't we, señor?'

'How neatly you express it.'

I shrugged. 'It's my trade you know. How perfectly *you* understand English. Nothing much escapes you, does it?

'That, señor,' he laughed, 'is *my* trade.'

I had set that one up for him in the knowledge that a chance to display his wit, like an opportunity to show off his medals, was bound to put him in good humour.

'You realise,' he told me, 'that in the course of your discussion with our mutual friend you must restrict yourself absolutely to literary matters?'

'You have my word of honour.'

'Sufficient as that is, you could hardly expect me to forgo the privilege of listening myself to such a brilliant conversation as this is likely to be.'

My heart sank; but I tried to hide my disappointment. I had considered the likelihood of the cell's being wired and I had thought of several ways of getting around this difficulty; but to have this clever chap right in there with us—'By all means,' I said with what I hoped was a nonchalant manner. 'Do you like Ortiz' poetry?'

'Superb!' Kissing his fingers—'that perfect felicity of phrasing with a dash of peon's sweat for savour! My friends tell me I recite pieces like the "Madrugada Roja" beautifully.'

He gestured toward the door, indicating that the man who had conducted me there was to open it. He stood aside and with another slight bow waved me inside the cell.

The small room was better furnished, I assumed, than the quarters for ordinary criminals. There was a bed and two chairs, a table beneath the high, barred window and a book case against one wall. Manuel Ortiz sat in one of the chairs with the light from the window falling on his tousled iron-grey hair. He looked up as we entered, show-ing me a dark, strong, deeply-seamed face. His nose had been broken and flattened; his mouth was wide with a hint of humour barely discernible at the very ends; his eyes were set back under thick grey brows and opaquely black, so that it would have been difficult ever to know what was really going on behind them. But it was his hands which made the greatest impression on me—thick-veined with stubby gnarled fingers and such a look of strength that, dangling idly between his knees as they were at that moment, they seemed to sum up the whole tragedy of this manacled giant.

He rose slowly to his feet and with the ghost of a smile at the edges of his mouth held out one of his powerful hands to me.

I clasped it firmly, looking at that dark, furrowed face with the same instant respect I had felt for El Huero; only this time the feeling went even deeper. In the short inter-val that our hands remained locked, I had the sense of being in direct touch with the great popular movements which were shaking our whole world into a different pattern

'You see, Ortiz,' the smooth voice of the prison officer intruded on these reflections, 'you have not only me as a devotee today but also a distinguished literary critic from our great neighbour to the north.'

I was more uneasy and embarrassed than if the man had suddenly lashed out at Manuel Ortiz with a whip.

Ortiz paid no attention to the man. To me he said in stiff and hesitant English : 'I am glad you have come. It could not have been easy for you to arrange. I have seen no one in many months.'

The prison officer chuckled. 'We couldn't have our great poet disturbed by all the tiresome people his genius would've attracted. We have tried to be discriminating on his behalf.'

I looked at the book case. 'I'm pleased to see you are permitted to read, Señor Ortiz.'

'That,' with a contemptuous look at the officer, 'was only put here yesterday. To impress you,' he added. He took out one of the volumes. 'A book on cookery is not very useful to me in my present situation.'

'Let me see that,' the prison official said angrily. But he quickly regained his attitude of supercilious composure. 'Alas, one's underlings in a place like this are illiterate louts. I shall see to it that the unsuitable volumes are replaced with the right sort of books.'

'Now?' Ortiz enquired with a half-humorous lift of heavy brows.

'Oh no, not now! I have explained that I would not for anything miss the conversation of two such notable literary gentlemen as yourselves.'

Manuel Ortiz motioned to me to sit down in the other chair as he resumed the posture in which I had found him, hands between his knees, forehead deeply wrinkled. 'Sometimes when I have been depressed, I have remembered the things you wrote about me, Señor Brandeis. It has encouraged me to think that even in the United States my voice has not been unheard.'

'Your poetry speaks for itself,' I assured him sincerely —'even in translation. There was nothing I could add by way of comment.' I glanced at the officer who leaned against the wall smiling smugly. How in the hell was I going to deliver any message with that oily bastard oozing all over the cell!

'There's another reason why I'm pleased to be able to see you,' I told Ortiz. 'I bring you warmest greetings from your friend, Rafael Gabaldon.'

'You have been to San Pedro?'

'I've come to the capital from there.'

'How is he, my old friend?'

'Well.'

'And the children, Juanito and Ana?'

'Also very well. They speak of you often.'

'They are like my own children, those two.'

'Yes,' I said, thinking desperately. 'You know that a new edition of your poems is coming out in the States.'

'I had not heard; but I am pleased.'

'Yes. I hope that we'll be able to make some improvements—finding better English equivalents of the more telling phrases, you know.'

Ortiz shook his head. 'It is always difficult, translating poetry from one language to another.'

'That's true. But it's easier when the poems are as charged with meaning as yours. It's the poets with a verbal facility but nothing much to say who are untranslatable.'

'But I make my poems for the poor peons of my country. For people in the States . . .' he shrugged. 'You see, I test every line by asking myself if it would say anything to my mother who could hardly read.'

'That's why they're universal,' I told him. 'Still, I admit that problems do arise. You remember in "Song of a Battered Sombrero" there's a verse . . .' I took out my pen and felt in my pockets. Then, of the officer I asked: 'Do you have a piece of paper?—anything I could write on.'

He produced an envelope doubtfully.

'That's fine,' I said quickly and took it from him. On the back I wrote a line I recalled from that famous poem; and underneath I put down the English version. 'You see,' handing it to Ortiz. 'That really misses the impact of the original.'

Ortiz read what I had written and nodded. When he handed it back, the officer leaned over my shoulder to have his own look.

'Or another example that's even more difficult,' I said. 'Toward the end you have this phrase.' I wrote the Spanish quickly and added: 'Sick bay. Four days. Orderly called Raimundo.' I passed it to Ortiz at once.

He read it and shook his head. 'You've quoted it wrong.'

'Of course.' I took it back and hurriedly scratched out the Spanish phrase and the few words in English. 'There,' when I had written the line again. 'For that we used the English expression, "Speaking through the mouth of his wound." But it's clumsy. We can do better next time.'

I crumpled up the envelope and looked about for a place to put it.

'If you please, señor.' The official took it from my hand.

I had expected that and I was fairly sure I had done a good job of marking out what I had written with my broad-nibbed pen. But had Ortiz understood that he was to find some way of getting himself into the sick bay in four days' time? I should have written it in Spanish; but it would have taken longer.

'I hope I shall see a copy of the new edition when it is ready,' Ortiz said.

I turned to the officer. 'If I send it here, will he receive it?'

'Certainly. We are not barbarians, señor. I trust I shall be permitted to read it also.'

'But of course,' I said magnanimously, 'I'll send you a copy as well.'

Ortiz and I talked generally for another quarter of an hour. The prison officer looked at his watch and explained that the visit must be brought to an end.

Ortiz stood up and held out his hand to me. 'Your

coming to see me has been like a long-awaited message from all my friends outside.'

'They long to be reunited with you,' I said.

'Perhaps the time will come.' And to the officer with a smile : 'What do you say to that?'

'Even though it would rob our prison of its chief claim to fame and me of a most distinguished acquaintance, I would welcome the order of your release, Ortiz.'

He opened the door of the cell and, with a last glance at that great man, I walked out into the corridor.

8

'A Favourable Exchange?'

THAT same afternoon, following El Huero's instructions, I scribbled on a piece of paper, the single word 'Libertad', put it in an envelope on which I wrote the name Francisco Lopez, and pushed the envelope through the letter slot of a block of flats in the Calle Segundo Mayo.

At nine o'clock I went to a little bar called the Caballo Blanco in a poor quarter of town but within sight of the office buildings and bright lights of the main centre.

I ordered a drink at the bar and asked the man who served me if he knew of anyone in the market for a 'sixty three Pontiac.

He gave me a drink and jerked his head toward a table in the corner where a man sat reading a newspaper. I took my glass over to this table.

'Lopez?' I enquired.

'Sit down, señor,' folding up the paper. 'You've seen our friend?'

'This afternoon. I think I got the message to him.'

'You *think* you did!'

'It was difficult. We weren't alone—not even for a moment. Still,' boasting a little—justifiably I felt, 'by the exercise of a certain cunning I believe I can say that I got across to him his part of the plan.'

'Are you sure enough for us to go ahead?'

'Well, yes.'

He looked at me searchingly and then he smiled. 'Bueno!'

'Our friend has four days to arrange by some means to be in the right place.'

'Well done, señor. This information will be passed on immediately.'

'I shall be remaining in the capital till I hear something, one way or the other. Our companions east of here thought it might look odd if I left as soon as I had seen the old man. I might even be of some further assistance if . . .'

He held up his hand in polite rejection. 'We were told you mustn't be mixed up in this any more than was necessary.'

'I kept my eyes open while I was inside.'

'I'm sure you did, señor. But we have friends in there who are taking care of all that.'

'Anyway, you know where to get in touch with me.'

'Yes.' He held out his hand. 'This is a fine thing you have done for the people of this country.'

'Shucks! It warn't nothing really.'

'Like in the cowboy pictures, eh, señor?' he laughed.

'That's me—a born vaquero. One day I'll find a horse born to recognise that fact.'

'And now, you'd better go. We don't want to run the risk of being seen together.'

I got up. 'Oh, by the way, what *about* that 'sixty-three Pontiac?'

'I'll trade you a horse for it,' he said with a wink.

'Can I sleep on it?'

When I got back to my hotel, there was a letter waiting for me. It was from Ana. She had not known my address; but she had given the letter to Juan to post for her.

My enjoyment at receiving the letter, the way I took it up to my room to savour it in privacy bothered me a bit. There had to be absolutely no wavering on my part if I was to avoid behaving badly. I had reached an age when it would be very flattering to have a young woman, particularly one as lovely as Ana, think of me romantically. And assuring myself that I could not possibly arouse any serious feelings was no excuse for fooling around. Girls can fall in love with almost anything if the circumstances conspire against them. I tore the letter up as an earnest of my firm intention not to take the slightest advantage of Ana just to appease my vanity. I had already messed up enough people's lives, not excluding my own.

The next few days I did succeed in writing several articles which I sent off to the printer. One descriptive piece on the floral splendours of the botanical gardens actually inspired me to spend an afternoon drifting about there. Generally speaking, I have lived my life in reverse order, first writing about something before being moved to try it out in practice and then deciding I should have left it as it appeared on the printed page. If I had not written that silly novel about love and marriage when I was a young man, I most probably would never have acquired all those tiresome wives.

That was very likely what gave my present adventures on the fringe of a group of revolutionaries their freshness and excitement. I had not written anything about such attempts to change society and therefore I was never sure what was coming next. It was like being a character in somebody else's book. I could only hope the author knew his business.

Each morning when I came down to breakfast, I glanced expectantly at the front page of the newspaper placed beside my plate. It was with something of the thrill I recalled from the first time I had ever seen something I had written in print that I read that Friday the headlines of Manuel Ortiz' escape from prison.

'So they pulled it off!' I exclaimed to myself, running my eyes down the column. 'And not without my help, of course.' Indeed, so conscious was I of having participated in the events behind the news story that it seemed to me every one else in the dining room must be staring at me.

I tried to imagine what Manuel Ortiz' face must have looked like when he found himself free after all those years in jail. I thought of how it would be when he saw old friends again, when he met the Gabaldons; and it brought a moistness to my eyes. I felt very proud to have been involved at all in the release of that wonderful old man. How people all over the country, all over Central America, must be rejoicing that someone who had spoken for them in unforgettable words was now at large—just as if the very spirit of freedom were once more loose in the land!

I had hardly finished breakfast when a policeman in uniform and a man in plain clothes entered the hotel looking for me.

I had been pretty sure they would want to interview me. I was the only visitor Ortiz had seen in a long while and it was bound to look suspicious that he had escaped shortly afterward. I was not particularly worried. What could they prove?

The man in the suit picked me out at once. 'Good morning, Señor Brandeis? There're some questions we'd like to ask you.'

'Certainly. I've been expecting you.'

'Then I hope we haven't kept you waiting.'

'Not at all. Is the lounge all right? or would you prefer to come up to my room?'

'We'll go to the Balbueno Police Station, if you don't mind.'

'But I do mind. Are you arresting me?'

'What for? Have you done something illegal?'

'Not that I know of.'

'Then what objection can you have to coming with us? You may be able to help in some enquiries we're making.'

'I could help just as well here and it would take less of my time.'

He pursed his lips. 'Could I see your passport, Señor Brandeis?'

'Well, I don't have one, I'm afraid.'

'Can I see your entry permit then?'

'My permission to enter was stamped in my passport.'

'Which you haven't got.'

'As a matter of fact, it was stolen from me.'

'I see. And naturally you reported its theft to your Embassy.'

'Well, I didn't like to bother them. I mean, it might've turned up again, mightn't it?'

The man smiled at his little victory. 'It's all very irregular, Señor Brandeis. I'm afraid I'll have to ask you to come to the Police Station after all. It shouldn't take us long to check whether you're in the country legally or not.'

'Okay,' I shrugged. 'You win.'

There was a black Ford police car outside the hotel. I got in the back with the man in the suit; and we drove off. I turned to wave out of the back window to the people who had come out on the porch to watch me being taken away.

'One mustn't forget one's public,' I explained.

'I hope they won't forget *you*,' he said in a tone I did not like.

'When we get to the Station, I assume I can telephone the British Embassy and let them know where I am?'

'Naturally.'

And after we had driven some distance, 'Is this the way to the Police Station?' I asked.

'It's one way—not, perhaps, the shortest.'

'But I recognise this road!' I exclaimed. 'It leads to the Federal Prison.'

'I thought you'd remember it, Señor Brandeis.'

'What's the big idea? Do you feel that there's some advantage in questioning me at the scene of the crime?'

'Whose crime?' he demanded.

'How should I know? I've merely read in the paper that Manuel Ortiz has escaped. That's what you want to question me about, isn't it?'

'We don't have to question you, Señor Brandeis. We *know* you delivered a message to Ortiz.'

'How can you prove it?' I asked, trying to keep my voice steady.

'You're the only one who's seen him. It had to be you who got word to him.'

'That's not proof,' I pointed out.

'It satisfies us.'

'Then you *are* arresting me?'

'How can we arrest you? As you say, we haven't any *proof* that you helped set up Ortiz' escape.'

'But you can't hold me *without* arresting me.'

'Why ever not, Señor Brandeis?'

'It's against the law, that's why.'

'Oh come now. It's the job of the police to uphold the law, isn't it? What we're doing must be legal, since we *are* the police.'

'I'm not even sure of that,' I muttered.

He reached inside his jacket and produced his official credentials. 'It's not a very flattering photograph; but it *is* me, you have to admit.'

'Very obliging,' I said sarcastically. 'And what about Habeas Corpus?'

'There's that, Señor Brandeis. If anyone challenged us to show reason why we were holding you, I suppose we'd have to let you go. But what if no one knows you're in our hands?'

'What about the people at the hotel?'

'I'm glad you mentioned that. You really mustn't sign false names on hotel registers, Señor Brandeis. Suppose someone wanted to find out what had become of you? It would be very confusing for him, wouldn't it?'

I sank back in temporary defeat. Then I thought of something else. 'I don't believe you'd hold me without any justification. I think you're trying to scare me to make me talk.'

'If you think that, then you've nothing to worry about, have you?'

I gave it up after that and remained silent during the rest of the drive to the prison.

'Do you sometimes get the feeling you've been in a place before?' I asked us we drove through the gates.

'Do *you* sometimes get the feeling you might not ever be anywhere else?' And with a smile: 'That's just to frighten you, of course.'

'Why don't you ask me some questions then? Why don't you ask me whom I was working for?'

'We know. Ribera.'

'Go on. Everything untoward that happens gets blamed on Ribera.'

'You know a lot about our political underground for a man who's only visiting the country as a tourist.'

'Well, people talk.'

'You should imitate them, Señor Brandeis. Where's El Huero these days?'

'Never heard of him.'

The man shrugged and as the car stopped he got out. Someone was waiting for us within the shadow of an arched doorway—the resplendently dressed official who had been present at my meeting with Ortiz.

'Señor Brandeis,' he greeted. 'I had no idea that we would have the privilege of another visit from you so soon.'

'You never know your luck, do you?' I said bitterly.

'And I believe this time you intend making a longer stay.'

'A man's got to get a bit of peace and quiet somehow.'

'I've a very pleasant surprise for you,' he told me. 'You can have the room in which we had such an interesting literary discussion.'

'Yes. I heard it was unoccupied now.'

'If you'll come with me.'

'Lead on, Admiral.' I turned to the plain-clothes man. 'I wouldn't like to be in your shoes when the congressman of my district learns of this.'

He smiled. 'This congressman, I take it, is one of the *Communist* members of the House of Representatives.'

'Very funny! You may not know it; but the U.S. government doesn't like people from the States being locked up for the views they hold. It reserves that prerogative for itself.'

'At least,' he said with a smile, 'you can be grateful that we have such a humane prison system. You obviously don't know about our arrangements for allowing wives to visit their husbands periodically in their cells.'

'If you call that humane, you obviously don't know my wives.'

'Of course, it doesn't apply to political prisoners.'

'Well, that's something.'

With a junior warden in attendance the officer led the way to the wing for politicos. The cell Ortiz had been in all those years was opened and I walked inside.

'It's a great relief to me,' the official told me in that unctuous voice I found so irritating, 'that I won't be without intelligent conversation, after all.'

126

'Doesn't it hurt your pride that you can only keep friends by putting them behind bars?'

'I'm a very humble man, Señor Brandeis. I'm content with what I can get in the way of companionship.'

I crossed to the book case. Everything was exactly as it had been on my previous visit.

'My duties call me away,' the official said, 'but I'll look in on you later. I hope you'll be comfortable here.'

'Sure,' taking out one of the books Ortiz had complained about. 'I can always brush up my knowledge of how to cook hot tamales. I don't suppose there'd be a recipe for file-filled cake.'

The door was slammed and the bolt shot home.

There was something very definitive about that sound. It gave me a good deal to think over. The simple fact was that Ortiz was out and I was in; and while I could see that for the people of this land it was a very favourable exchange, I could not honestly have said that I was able to identify myself with their point of view completely.

I wondered if those who had persuaded me to take a hand in Ortiz' escape had realised that it would probably end like this. One could argue that even if they *had* known, the stakes were so great and the issues so important that they would be justified in sacrificing one small-time literato; but, again, I could not entirely see the matter in that light myself.

Perhaps my captors had some hope that they could use me as a bargaining counter for the return of Ortiz; but my friends, if that was not too strong a term for them under the circumstances, would be crazy to enter into such a deal. I could imagine that Ortiz, left to his own devices, might prefer to give himself up than to have another man incarcerated in his place; but I could also think of a lot of good reasons I could have produced myself to dissuade him from such a quixotic act.

No, any way one looked at it, the inescapable conclusion seemed to be that Kyle Brandeis had fallen an early and not very willing victim in one of Central America's national liberation struggles. There was a certain historical justice in that, I had to admit, since my country of adoption was exploiting the people outrageously and through its puppets, into whose hands I had fallen, continued to run the place in its own interests. But I could not help thinking that the justice of it would have been more perfect if, instead of a wet liberal like myself who at least had some of the right ideas, this cell could have contained one of the Administration 'hawks' or, perhaps, a director of one of the big corporations or, at the very least, a native-born Yankee!

I paced up and down the cell, looked out of the barred window, sat down on the edge of the hard cot. It was not a place I was ever going to get out of by my own efforts. Would those outside try to devise some means of freeing me? It would not be easy after Ortiz' escape. I supposed I could wait a few days and pretend to be ill just to see what opportunities might still exist in the sick bay. Pretending to be ill would be easy enough, anyway. I felt sick already!

Eventually I heard the bolt of my door withdrawn and lunch was brought in by one of the attendants.

It was not very good. I did not think I could have given the Federal Prison even one star in any tourist guide I might some day compile—in my declining years on present evidence.

When the remains had been taken away, I lay down on the cot to see if I could not sleep off a few hours out of the infinite number stretching drearily away ahead of me. I found myself thinking of Ana. I kept getting brief glimpses of her in this pose or that—nothing so satisfying as a full-face view, but the tantalising curve of cheek as she gazed down over the orchard of orange trees that first evening at the hacienda or the sweet line of her forearms as her hands rested on the saddle horn the day we rode along the little stream.

Well, at any rate, the question of what I was going to do about Ana was no longer very pressing. I tried to get a different perspective on my imprisonment by thinking up all the other problems which being locked up virtually eliminated. There were all those women I was supporting back in the States. Imagining their fury if they knew that I had gone and got myself thrown in jail, thereby cutting off all future payments of alimony, was as close as I could come to being reconciled.

The afternoon was broken by a visit from that splendid uniform which had the prison officer inside it.

'I thought I would look in on you, Señor Brandeis, in case time was lying on you a bit heavily.'

'I'm not *that* bored,' I told him frankly.

'Of course, you haven't even finished one day yet,' he reminded me callously.

'Tell me something,' I asked out of curiosity. 'Is my having been picked up and put here official? or is it something cooked up between you and that other smooth character in the local equivalent of a Brook Brothers' suit?'

'That's an interesting question, señor.'

'It's the answer that interests me more.'

'The answer, I'm afraid, isn't simple. You ask if your being here is official.' And with a florid gesture : 'It is and, again, it isn't.'

'Thanks !'

'What I mean is that it's official in the sense that no one involved in placing you here has exceeded his author-ity and is likely to be punished for unwarranted zeal. But on the other hand, it's unofficial in the sense that no one in government circles could be charged with knowing that an inmate of this prison had arrived without passing through the usual legal channels.'

'Very convenient for everyone—except me perhaps.'

'It's often politically necessary for a government not to let its right hand know what its left hand is doing.'

'Particularly when one of those hands is usually in somebody else's pocket.'

'You're fond of jokes, señor.'

'I prefer them, though, when they're not on me. Isn't somebody going to start questioning me about whom I've been working with, what they're planning to do next and all that? This is too much like waiting in a dentist's outer office to suit me.'

'I assure you, I came here to talk to you about literature, about the things of the soul.'

'Well, I think you ought to know that *subtle* tortures aren't going to get you anywhere. I'm much too coarse-grained for anything more sophisticated than a rack.'

'You're much too *cocky,* señor,' he said with a thoroughly unpleasant smile. 'But time cures all faults, doesn't it?'

'Suppose you come back then when I'm cured, which' —loosening my collar—'in a place as hot as this, oughtn't to take long.'

I slept fitfully that night and during the next day saw no one at all but the orderly who brought my food.

Just before dusk on the day after that, the door of my cell was opened and the plain-clothes man who had picked me up at the hotel came in. He was accompanied by a policeman in uniform with the customary revolver in an ornately-stamped holster.

'I've been checking up on you, Señor Brandeis.'

'Then you know that I entered this country legally— and I'm prepared to leave the same way, right now.'

He regarded me thoughtfully. 'We never doubted that, you know. I mean, I've been checking up on your past.'

'Makes pretty dull reading, I'm afraid; but I didn't have you in mind at the time.'

'It appears that you've been associated with various left-wing groups. You came down here to stir up trouble, didn't you?'

'I came down here to get *out* of trouble; but I don't seem to have managed things very well. Still, if you think I'm just a goddamned nuisance, as I said, I'm perfectly ready to be thrown out on my ear.'

'Not so fast,' he grinned. 'I'd like to ask you a few questions.'

Well, I thought, we had finally got to it. All alike, these 'mañana' countries—always putting things off.

'Whatever views you may have held in the States, Señor Brandeis, you must admit you had no right to come here and act on them in *our* country.'

'Well, I wasn't exactly encouraged to act on them there, either.'

His look got tougher. 'Who was responsible for your coming here?'

'Two people,' I answered truthfully.

He took out a note-book and prepared to write down the names. 'Go on.'

'My first and, also, my second wives. Didn't you come across them when you were checking up on my past? I was just about to ask *you* what they're up to now.'

He put the note-book in his pocket and, suddenly, slapped me across the face with the back of his hand. It was so quick and made me so angry that I took a step toward him without having time to think how foolish it was.

The policeman grabbed me and pinioned my arms behind me.

'Now,' the man said coldly, 'perhaps we can continue this interview in a serious manner.'

I could feel a tickle at the corner of my mouth which was probably blood.

'In San Pedro you were in touch with a family called Gabaldon,' he pointed out. 'Whom else did you meet there?'

'Well now, there was a Mrs. Winscomb, from Ohio I believe; a man called Homer Findley who wore . . .'

He slapped me in the face again. 'You know what I mean. Who told you about the plan to get Ortiz out of prison?'

'I don't know what you're talking about. I came to the capital partly to see Manuel Ortiz in connection with a new edition. I arranged my interview with him quite openly through the American Embassy and your Minister of Culture. If I'd known anything about a projected escape, I'd hardly have hung around to be picked up by you.'

'You're lying,' he shouted at me. 'Don't think we can't make you tell us the truth. Show him, Garcia.'

The policeman jerked one of my arms up behind my back and began to apply pressure.

'Did you meet a man called El Huero?'

'Christ!' I exclaimed as my arm was forced up higher.

'*Did* you?' he shouted at me again.

I was in too much pain to speak. I shook my head in denial and my arm was given another wrench upwards.

My head was bent low on my chest. Sweat prickled on my forehead and ran down my face. I tried to catch my breath and let out an involuntary groan.

'Did you meet El Huero?' he screamed at me.

The cell was swimming and I felt nauseously faint. I still managed a weak shake of my head.

At a sign from my interrogator the policeman released his hold and I sank to my knees.

'We'll be back,' the man said threateningly. 'You'd better make up your mind to tell us what we want to know.' He half turned away and then, pivoting back on the ball of one foot, kicked me hard in the chest with the other.

I lay on my back on the floor of the cell for some time after I heard the bolt thrown.

I had occasionally speculated on the subject of how much pain a man could endure without betraying his companions or some cause he believed in. If there was a limit, varying from individual to individual, beyond which it was impossible not to spill one's guts, it had always seemed to me irrational to go through the earlier stages of torture. But in the event one was *not* rational about it. Such an assault on one's person called up a kind of throttled fury which made one unreasonably determined never to give in—whatever they did. The very fact that the bastard who had struck me wanted so badly to know what I could tell him gave me a sense of pleasure in the knowledge that he was never going to find out. To hell with him!

I got up painfully and rolled over on the cot. A doubt occurred to me. Would I be *able* to hold out? Perhaps excessive pain over a long period changed one into someone else on whom one's present will would have no control. In spite of myself I began to think of all the really horrible things that could be done to one's body.

There was a sharp rap as the bolt on the door was flung back.

'Oh no!' as my heart seemed to sink down to the pit of my stomach and throb there achingly. 'They can't have come back so soon!'

The door flew open. I raised fearfully on one elbow and there, standing in the entrance, a broad smile on his freckle-dark face showing the strong white teeth, was El Huero.

'Thank Christ!' I sighed.

9

'You Can Stop Talking. You're Dead'

I DID not know how in the world El Huero had penetrated this fortress of a prison and unlocked the door of my cell; but one thing I was sure of—no man in all the annals of history was ever greeted with greater warmth and relief than he was at that particular moment in time.

'Thank Christ you've come!' I rushed forward and gripped his hand. 'I can't imagine how you managed it; but the flowers in May aren't in it when it comes to being welcome.'

'You look as though you've been pushed around a bit.'

'It's only the beginning. The bastards were coming back later to do a real job on me.'

'You didn't tell them anything?' he asked quickly.

'Not a thing.'

'Nice going, Kyle.'

'Let's get the hell out of here—if it's possible.'

'That's the idea.' He motioned me to silence and stepped back into the corridor.

I followed him out of the cell and saw, standing on each side of the door, the two well-armed bodyguards who had been with him before. I smiled at them like old friends. The one carrying a carbine nodded; the other took a dead cigar from between his teeth to grin.

El Huero led the way and the three of us fell in behind him. We crossed the footway to the other block and started down the dark stairs.

What had they done, I wondered—killed every guard

in the place? I did not see anyone about at all.

The courtyard too was empty. One of the El Huero's bodyguards drew his revolver as we went out through the doorway and moved along the face of the building in thick shadow.

El Huero signalled us into a kind of alcove as a searchlight briefly swept the open area between the block and the main gate. In the blacker night succeeding the glare we ran across the court and flattened ourselves against the high wall to be out of range of the observation tower.

I was breathing heavily from all this exertion and excitement coming so soon after being worked over by those damned policemen; but along with my physical discomfort went another kind of disquiet. There was something very puzzling about this break-out.

El Huero tapped the shoulder of the man with the carbine who inched along with his back to the wall till he was close to the gate.

There was a minute or so of utter silence, then we heard our man give a sharp order in a lowered voice. A moment later he summoned us to the gate.

Two prison guards stood with their hands raised, a third had his hands on the lever that opened the massive doors mechanically.

El Huero's other shadow moved past me quickly and jammed his cocked revolver into the back of this man at the controls. 'Open up!'

With a creaking that sounded enormous in the general quiet the doors began to swing ponderously outward. As soon as the gap was sufficient, El Heuro and I slipped through, followed closely by the other two who backed away still covering the gate with carbine and revolver.

'Just like that!' I whispered sceptically. 'I'd like to know how in the hell you got inside to begin with.'

El Huero did not answer. 'Come on,' he urged; and

the four of us ran down a gentle slope and plunged through the brush bordering a grove of eucalyptus trees.

It was an extensive stand of trees and we groped our way through them for perhaps half an hour before coming out into a field where three or four horses shied away in the darkness from our approach. There was a narrow irrigation canal at the other side of the field and beyond that an unpaved road—little more than a track I discovered when we turned down it.

Some six or seven hundred yards along this dirt road we came to a black Buick saloon parked to one side. El Huero unlocked the door and turned on the headlights. He went around to the front of the car and standing in the twin beams beckoned to me to join him.

I stepped forward and faced him, frowning slightly both from the glare and from my perplexity as to what he was up to.

He moved around so that his back was to the car, leaving me blinking in the full blaze of the front lamps. I could not see either of the other men but I knew that they stood on either side of the glowing beams which flooded over me and dissipated themselves in the blackness far down the road.

'Just like the third degree,' I said with an unconvincing smile.

'We couldn't leave you in that prison,' El Huero told me after a pause. 'Too dangerous.'

'Naturally, I'm damned glad to get out of there; but,' I assured him, 'I wouldn't have talked.'

'You might have started thinking though. There must be limits even to your stupidity.'

It was like a slap in the face. I must have recoiled slightly, just as when that plain-clothes man had backhanded me a few hours ago.

'I don't think I . . .'

'Shut up! I haven't much time. The simple fact is that you were bound to realise sooner or later what I've been doing.'

'Like Watson?' the idea popped into my head.

'Like Watson. So, like Watson, you had to be got rid of.'

'I still don't . . .'

'I'm working with the Central Intelligence Agency.' And with an unpleasant chuckle: 'You may have heard of us.'

'I've heard of you,' I said in a lifeless tone. Then, out of a kind of angry despair, I added: 'I've heard of the Gestapo too. They're not around any more.'

'We're different. We're around—I mean *all* around too.'

'I don't believe it. You! El Huero! the great friend of Mexican labourers! The man whose name is known all over Central America!'

'That's me,' he grinned. 'And when this job's over I'll still be the people's friend—in on the beginnings of a popular revolt somewhere else.'

I stared at him incredulously. Even though it was the only possible explanation of everything that had been puzzling me, I still couldn't take it in. I searched that face which was largely obscured in shadow, looking for some break in the dark mask. I said, almost pleadingly: 'You're kidding, aren't you, Barry? This is some kind of joke.'

He took something from the inside pocket of his coat and held it so that the car lights illuminated it—his C.I.A. identification booklet.

'I'll show you something else.' He brought out my passport with the traveller's cheques still held between the pages.

As I reached out for it, he laughed and tore up both passport and cheques, throwing the pieces at my feet.

That takes some doing when the passport is British.

'But I don't understand,' shaking my head in blank dismay. 'When did they win you over?'

He laughed again. 'Win me over! I've been working for them for years.'

'In California, when you helped organise the fruit-pickers?'

'Of course. Who do you think put the finger on the commie militants among those labourers? I don't mind telling you all this because you're going to die tonight.'

'You mean you could kill me in cold blood!'

'It's got to be done. I have to wind this whole business up in the next few days and you'd get in my hair.'

My eyes narrowed speculatively. 'Why do you bother to tell me at all—since I'm to be bumped off anyway?'

'I'll answer that one. There's one disadvantage about my calling; I can never boast of my successes. In fact, the better I am at my job the more unlikely it becomes that people will ever know just how good I am. Well now, it amuses me to brag a little before you—you, particularly; and do you know why?'

I did not say anything. I was really too horrified to speak.

'I'll tell you why. Partly because you're a writing man. You must be thinking this moment what a story my life would make. Of course, in a way I regret that you won't be able to write my biography; but,' with that laugh which had once struck me as so frank and free, 'my regret at such a lost opportunity must be a little thing compared to yours, eh? And that's not the only reason. I can't help remembering the look of—well, almost devotion whenever we met. That's true, isn't it? You'd have done anything for me. I had only to suggest this or that and you fell all over yourself in your eagerness to carry it out. Your admiration has been one of the greatest credits I've ever received. I couldn't let you die without expressing my appreciation, could I?'

'You're wrong there,' I ground out in a voice trembling with fury. 'It wasn't you I was ready to serve in any way possible. It was the things I thought you stood for. You! You're nothing. A hireling of everything that's corrupt and reactionary.'

'Don't give *me* that left-wing eyewash. I'm a patriot. I serve my country—without even expecting any recognition for it. What're you? An amateur traitor that's all. I only wish all the enemies of the United States were as hopeless bunglers as you are.'

'You're a liar. You don't serve your country. You serve the clique that wages war all over the world to keep the profits rolling in. You're one of those who make the name of the United States stink in one country after another. You're . . .'

He cut me off abruptly. 'You can stop talking, Brandeis. You're dead.'

I looked down at my fists, clenched tight in the car lights and showing white across the knuckles. I had been about to hit him, even though I knew it would only end things more quickly by inviting a bullet out of the darkness. I *should* have hit him and I loathed myself for my cowardice. I had never detested myself so much—fool, clown, coward. To have been taken in so easily by that cheap gangster who tried to wrap himself in an American flag! It was my cursed vanity that had done it. If I had thought for a moment, I ought to have realised that no serious revolutionaries would have anything to do with an incompetent buffoon like myself. All this agony of self-hatred while I stood there with my nails cutting into my palms and Jones looking me up and down with a self-satisfied contempt.

'Rómulo! José!' he suddenly called. 'Take him away. Conceal the body well.'

There were murmurs of assent from outside the beam of light.

'I'm driving to San Pedro straight away,' Jones told them. 'You two can take the first train back tomorrow. Make sure the body won't be found. There's a stream over there which might be useful for hiding it.'

As he went around to the door on the left side, I yelled after him: 'May the curses of every poor peon in this land follow you to your grave!'

He laughed and got inside. The door slammed and the engine started; but he did not back onto the roadway till the two men had moved into the lights and grabbed hold of me.

The one who carried a revolver and was never without a cigar looped one hand in my belt at the back and jabbed the muzzle of his gun into my side.

'Just walk on, señor,' he said.

I heard the car drive away and stumbled forward over the uneven ground. It was very dark, pitch black for me after staring into the headlights.

I could feel the man's knuckles digging into my back and the steady pressure of the revolver. There was not a chance of trying to break away and make a run for it, though the heaviest odds would have been worth risking.

'Well,' I almost shrugged, 'this is it. This is the way it ends.' My eyes moistened—as if I were shedding tears for someone else about to die. It was that sort of pity—rather detached, just as if I myself would go on being aware of all the things some poor fellow who was to fall under the guns of two thugs in this small country would never do now, all the people he would never see again. I felt sick and miserable that a life was to be broken off thus mean-

141

inglessly, with no hope any more that somehow some sort of sense might still be made of it.

'That way, señor.' The fist at my back guided me down to the right.

That curious politeness struck an odd note under the circumstances. I wondered how I was going to behave in the last few moments before the shots were fired—still with that sense of detachment, as if I would be watching myself standing there in the night as the guns were levelled at my chest. Perhaps the certainty of death numbed one's sensibilities, I thought—so that it always seemed like something happening to someone else. Would that strange anaesthesia stay with me to the end? I felt very tired and sleepy—an exhaustion which made it extremely difficult to drag one foot after another. If I could only go quietly, in the depths of this doped dreaminess; but the shooting would be so noisy, I thought fearfully. Or maybe one did not hear anything at all when the guns went off.

'Stop here.'

We were under a large tree and I could hear water rippling somewhere ahead of us.

I was released and a hand on my shoulder turned me around and pressed me back against the trunk. My eyes were more accustomed to the dark now and I could see the two of them, though indistinctly. I could not tell what expressions were on their faces; and this pleased me in some obscure way—possibly because I felt it gave *me* a kind of discreet privacy in my last moments.

The man who had pushed me ahead of him returned the revolver to his holster while he took out a cigar and lit it, the match lighting their faces too briefly for me to make out anything but the black opaque eyes fixed on me intently.

The cigar end glowed as he inhaled. Then he glanced

at his companion who nodded and flicked the safety catch of the carbine.

I closed my eyes and then opened them. It had suddenly become terribly important to decide whether to keep my eyes open or closed and I did not know which was better.

The carbine began to come up and the hand of the man with the cigar between his teeth moved toward the butt of his revolver.

Then a very strange thing happened. That hand moving toward the holstered gun quickened, lifted the revolver and in a smooth upward sweep fired twice. I did not realise what had happened till the other man dropped the carbine, took one stumbling step forward and fell face down.

Even then I did not understand what was going on and waited for the revolver to be turned on me.

But the gun was shoved back into its holster and the man took the cigar out of his mouth and grinned.

My knees gave way then and I sat down heavily with my back against the tree.

The man laughed and it was the most beautiful sound I had ever heard. 'Too close, eh?' he said.

'Too goddamned close,' I sighed.

'I wanted to tell you it was all right. But José was beside me all the time.' He put out his hand and helped me to my feet.

'You're Rómulo then,' I said inanely.

'Yes. I knew I'd have to kill José some day. There're Mexicans like that, señor.'

'And there're Americans like El Huero. Too damned many of them. But how did you come to be working with him?'

'I knew him in the old days, in the San Fernando Valley. I helped him do some bad things there. But when I got back here, to a country like my own, it was different.

143

El Huero arranged for me to join Ribera's band as his own man; but I listened to what Ribera said about a land which would be ours one day and pretty soon I did not belong to El Huero any more.'

'You know what he's going to do, don't you? He's going to turn the armoury at Melina into a trap. When our friends raid it, there'll be a massacre.'

He nodded. 'We have to warn them. I'll catch a train back to San Pedro tomorrow.'

'Have you mentioned to anyone what you know about El Huero?'

'No, señor, I haven't. I should have; but, you see, he knows of a killing I did in the States for which I could be extradited and probably executed. It seemed better to wait for the right time and kill him myself.'

I had been thinking while he talked. 'I believe I'll start for San Pedro tonight. I don't want to go into the capital again. It's better that we don't travel together, anyway. And if two of us are trying, each on his own, to get word back in time . . .'

'It doubles our chances of success? Yes, that's a good plan. He's a very dangerous man, that El Huero. I know. I've seen what he can do.'

'To say nothing of the fact that he has the government, the police and the whole of the armed services on his side.'

Rómulo went over to the body sprawled on the ground and took a pistol out of the coat pocket. 'Can you use a gun, señor?' holding it out to me.

'I'd better learn to.'

'Here. I show you. Flip the catch with your thumb like that. Then just point and bang!'

He rummaged in José's pocket again and brought out a handful of cartridges. 'You try it when you get a chance.'

I stuck the revolver in my belt under my shirt. 'Do you

suppose any of the others with Ribera are really working
with El Huero?'

'I don't know. We'll have to find out, and kill them too.'

'How do I get to the highway which goes around south
of the lake and leads to San Pedro?'

'Follow that little road till it crosses a paved one. There
you turn right and go on for about a mile. Then you
meet the highway.'

'Let's go then.'

'Right, señor.'

'Should we do anything about him?' I asked with a
glance at José.

'Too late now.'

'I mean, hide the body?'

'Not necessary. Poor peons with guns die all the time
in this country. Nobody takes any notice. Norte Ameri-
canos are different.'

We walked back to the dirt road. Rómulo went to the
left, to get a bus which would take him back to the capital.
Before taking my own way to the right I called after him:
'Thanks, Rómulo. I know why you saved my life; but
I'm personally grateful all the same.'

He stopped and lit a cigar. 'It's nothing, señor. Life is
cheap in this land.'

'But mine is dear to me. You look out for yourself.
You're needed in San Pedro.'

'If anyone tries to stop me,' he grinned, 'I may have to
kill him.'

Very soon, I thought, as I strode along the rutted road,
there would not be a low-price hotel in the country which
did not have a pair of pajamas and a toothbrush of mine,
left behind when I had to get out of this town or that in
a hurry.

But beneath such random reflections I was really thinking about El Huero. Nothing in my life had ever shaken

me like that scene in the headlights of the car. I felt that
I would never again be sure of another human being as
long as I lived. If someone who had completely convinced
you he was everything a man ought to be, could suddenly
reveal a character so calculatingly vicious that the virtues
he pretended to have were spitting in humanity's face—
well, where were you? if not in some nightmare existence
in which the very people you thought you knew best were
always capable of any infamy! The dearest woman in
your life, as easily as kissing you tenderly, could stick a
knife between your ribs. The friend you had cherished
most of your days might prove to have been responsible
for every calamity that had ever befallen you.

I came to the crossing which had been described to me
and turned to the right, so deep in these gloomy thoughts
that I hardly noticed the distance I had covered.

With an involuntary shudder I tried to shake off that
evil fancy of a world in which you never really knew anything about anyone, telling myself that it was only a reac-
tion to the night's horrid events. But still, I found that
I did not feel quite the same about anyone any more—
not even Ana. I supposed I would be haunted for the rest
of my life by the thought that any smile *could* always
turn into a leer, any amiably outstretched hand *might*
conceal a cut-throat razor.

I hated El Huero as much for doing that to me as for
his betrayal of sincere people honestly fighting to make
this a better country for all those millions who had been
trampled on for centuries. I wanted desperately to see him
go down as José had dropped with those two slugs in him
—killed with no more compunction than one would shoot
a rattlesnake. Only his death would remove the treacher-
ous danger he represented to those I regarded as my
comrades. Only his death would wipe out the deepest
personal affront I could imagine—to have my best feel-

ings so perverted that they had been made to serve the interests I most abhorred. I had been foolish it was true, but out of generous motives. I did not think I deserved to have been made such a contemptible tool.

I stopped for a moment under the full realisation of what I was doing. I was going back to San Pedro solely to kill Barry Jones. I had parted with Rómulo willingly because I had to kill him myself. I was taking this chance of getting to San Pedro first because I did not want anyone to reach Jones before me. I would be miserable the rest of life if I did *not* kill him. I was terribly afraid of him. He was stronger and cleverer than I; and I doubted if I would have the courage to face him. But I also knew I would have no qualms at all about shooting him in the back.

I shook my head in a kind of surprise that there should have been this vindictive being inside me all along without my ever having known about it. Apparently the sense that people I thought I knew might at any time shock me with some entirely alien response would have to include myself.

Quickening my pace along the paved road I topped a gentle rise and saw lights ahead. There was a small garage where this road intersected the main highway.

That suited me very well because I did not think much of my chances of thumbing a ride at night. It would be better to try to talk some driver into giving me a lift when he pulled up for petrol.

It was only half past ten. I had thought it must be considerably later than that. I did not see how so much dread and anger and mortification could have been squeezed into so short a space of time.

I approached the little station from the front so that the attendant slumped on a bench near the pumps would not get any wrong ideas about me. I made up a story to

explain my plight, realising that things had got to a fine
state when one had to tell lies because the truth was quite
incredible; and the man invited me to share the bench
with him.

The third or fourth car to stop was driven by a business
man who was going to the coast and would be glad to rest
a bit while I spelled him at the wheel. According to the
map the attendant had showed me, this would take me
within some thirty miles of San Pedro.

I was not at all sleepy and the highway was good
enough to travel at speed. Several times the man asked me
to take it easy. Whenever I thought of El Huero, who
had probably driven along this same road, my foot
pressed harder on the accelerator.

About three in the morning we came to a sign post
indicating a road leading off to San Pedro. I tried to talk
the man into taking me at least part of the way along this
road; but he was not willing to do so. He finally lent me
a hundred pesos to get rid of me, letting me have the
name of his hotel in the coastal town without really be-
lieving he would ever see the money again. It never
occurred to me that I could have used my newly-acquired
gun to threaten him.

There was an almost full moon and I would possibly
have enjoyed hiking along the road if it were not for the
urgency driving me. There was no traffic to speak of and I
walked on for the best part of an hour without much
hope of getting a ride.

I was becoming more and more convinced that the
existing guide books were useless for anyone seeing the
country as I was doing. What was wanted was a good
practical handbook describing the jails which served the
best food and were easiest to escape from, the roads which
afforded the greatest likelihood of thumbing lifts and the
hotels which were prepared to look after one's personal

belongings when one had bolted without paying the bill. If I came through the next few days I might seriously consider filling this gap. I had a good start on collecting the necessary material already.

By the time a barking dog announced my arrival at a small cluster of houses I was getting desperate. I picked a door at random and banged on it. Some minutes later it was opened by a sleepy looking man whose annoyance I bought off by peeling a couple of pesos off the wad I had borrowed. There *was* a car in the village and he showed me the house of its owner.

The rest of the money persuaded the man who possessed the ancient van to drive me to San Pedro.

Dawn was just beginning to break when I told him to stop several miles short of town and got out. I waved to the man as he turned back along the road and then set out cross country to approach the town from the hill behind the Hotel *Buena Vista*.

I had passed a petrol drum half buried in the ground when I paused and turned back to it. I paced off forty or fifty feet, tugged at the revolver which stuck in my belt, freed it eventually and pointing at the drum pulled the trigger. Nothing happened. I had forgotten to release the safety catch.

I tried again, snap-shooting as I had seen them do in the movies. The bullet kicked up dirt at least three yards away from the drum. It made a hell of a racket, though. The *noise* might be disconcerting—but not of course to someone like El Huero. I gave up the idea of speed and sighted down the barrel, squeezing the trigger slowly till the damned thing went off. It was better than the first shot anyway. A very fat unarmed man who was prepared to stay perfectly still would have some pretty uneasy moments when I opened up.

I slipped the catch back to safe and hefted the gun by

149

the barrel. It would make a good club if I could sneak up behind the person to whom I had taken a dislike.

I replaced the spent cartridges and stuck the revolver, a Smith and Wesson thirty-eight, back into my belt, tastefully arranging my shirt to cover it. Still, it was a good idea to have disabused myself of any false confidence in my weaponry, I decided. As Siva is quoted as saying in the Gita : to be forewarned is to be four armed. I could certainly have done with a couple of extra hands in the task I had set myself.

10

'It's Not Your Country'

THE sun was just edging up over the horizon when I came out on the brow of the hill behind the hotel. Below me was the Gabaldon house with regularly planted orange trees sloping down to the edge of town, the buildings of San Pedro lying along the valley and the tops of the twin towers of the cathedral catching the first rosy light.

There were things I needed from the belongings I had left at the hotel; but I did not dare go there. I had to make contact with some of those involved in the conspiracy; but I did not know how to set about that either. When I had first become aware, quite accidentally, that there *was* some sort of plot afoot, I had gone through a period of looking at absolutely everyone I met and wondering if he, too, were not somehow mixed up in it. Now I was engaged in running over in my mind all the people I knew were in this scheme and trying to decide which of them were secretly working with El Huero; and, again, everyone I thought of, for all I knew, might be a U.S. or local agent.

On the whole, considering the mistakes I had made when I *had* begun to put confidence in this person or that, the safest course was to assume that every single individual *was* El Huero's man while knowing that, over all, his confederates could only be a small proportion of the whole revolutionary group.

When I made up my mind about what immediate

action to take, I hoped it was what I ought sensibly to do as well as what I wanted to do.

I walked down the hill, went around the hotel and crossed the road leading to town. From the back, near the stable, I entered the yard behind the Gabaldon hacienda. That paved terrace running the length of the house, those two ornamental urns in the morning sunlight made me look down at myself as a highly unsuitable object in my present state to be cluttering up the grounds.

Half hidden behind a cypress I studied the rear elevation of that gleaming white house and wondered whether I should wait for some glimpse of Ana or take more active steps to find her. From what I knew of her I tried to decide whether she was likely to be an early riser or not.

But time was pressing and I was bound to take minor risks in getting things moving at all. I climbed the stone stairs leading up to the tile-roofed court set back in the house like an open-sided patio. The door was unlocked, which must have meant that someone was up, anyway.

I slipped quietly inside and crossed the large room which looked out over the town. Listening at the door leading into the hall I could hear voices, one of them Ana's. She was saying something to her mother and her words became more distinct as she came into the hall.

I opened the door and put my finger on my lips as she saw me. Her eyes widened in surprise and concern; but she did not say anything.

She came closer and I whispered : 'I must see you.'

'Wait for me in the stable,' she said. 'There won't be anyone there at this time of day.'

I was renewing my acquaintanceship with Pedro when she came into the stable with a basin of warm water and some things wrapped in a towel.

'I know I'm filthy,' I said; 'but getting spruced up isn't a major consideration just now.'

'Hold still,' she commanded, dipping an edge of the towel in the water. 'There's blood on your mouth. I want to see how badly you're hurt.'

'It's nothing,' I insisted.

'Be quiet. This is going to sting.' She dabbed at the cut with a bit of cotton soaked in iodine.

'Ouch! I'm surprised your household isn't equipped with the new wonder-drug, metazone, which doesn't sting, sweetens the breath and is also excellent for clearing stopped-up drains.'

'I've never heard of it.'

'That's the trouble with these backward countries.' And when she had finished her ministrations: 'You're a remarkable woman, Ana. Anyone else would've been hurling questions at me so fast, I'd have been overwhelmed.'

'You'll explain what you want to when you get around to it.'

I shook my head in admiration. 'Tell me, Ana, do you trust me?'

'So much so I'm beginning to think that I've lost all my appeal.'

'Well, I didn't mean quite that. Would you do several things for me without demanding to know, at this stage, what it's all about?'

She looked at me very directly with those lovely dark eyes and said: 'You know I would, Kyle.'

That look bothered me and with a slight frown: 'I don't mean just on personal grounds.'

'I don't either,' she said seriously. 'I could never *have* any personal feelings about someone I didn't trust in other ways. I'm a patriot, too, Kyle.'

'I believe that.' I reached out and took her hand. 'I've got to see Juan—just as quickly as you can manage it.'

'I'll get him,' she told me simply.

153

'I need hardly tell you that no one must know I'm here
—not even Juan till he actually sees me. You'll have to
get him here some way without explaining why.'

She thought about it a moment before saying: 'All
right.' Then she added: 'You need clothes, too—and
probably something to eat.'

'Later. I've got to see Juan at once. A very great deal
indeed depends on it.'

'Wait here'; and without another word she was gone.

I was all right as long as I was on the move, as long as I
was doing something. In moments of inaction it was different. I kept imagining all the ways in which El Huero
might learn that I was still alive and all the things he
could do to rectify this little hitch in his plans.

I did not like being in that stable. It was too easy to
sneak up on it from various directions. From time to time
I did a round of the place, peering through the cracks in
the wooden doors, glancing out from behind the sacking
hanging over the open windows—rather like, I supposed,
a single frantic soldier trying to man a whole blockhouse.

'Quiet, boy,' I said soothingly to Pedro when he started
getting fidgety himself. 'Whose side are you on, anyway?'

At last I gave up any pretence of not being scared to
death and climbed the ladder to the loft where I could
cower behind some bales of hay and let myself go com-
fortably to pieces. I wished I had a cigarette. I took the
Smith and Wesson out of my belt and stared at it to see if it
would do anything for my morale. It did not. There were
two ways of looking at a gun, I thought, as I shifted it
from hand to hand: it gave you a peculiar distinction in
relation to everyone who did not have one; but it also
practically amounted to a challenge to everyone else who
did. It was the highly provocative nature of this latter
aspect of possessing a weapon which was most pressingly
with me at the time. I hastily stuck the gun back into the

top of my trousers and covered it again with my shirt, on the theory that a *concealed* weapon at least had the effect of smudging these issues.

An hour or so later I heard the doors of the stable open and peeping over the top of one of the bales I saw Ana enter with Juan. I waved to them sheepishly from the loft and climbed down.

'I'll leave you two,' Ana said, 'while I get something for you to eat, Kyle, and some clothes too. Do you want anything from the hotel?'

'No. Don't go to the hotel. It'll get around that I'm in the neighbourhood.'

When his sister had left, Juan asked me: 'What's happened to you?'

I studied him a moment before countering with a question of my own. 'What've you *heard* has happened to me?'

'Only that you helped get Ortiz out of jail.'

'Nothing else?'

'Nothing. I assumed you'd be coming back here, but I didn't expect you to turn up like this.'

'There've been times when I didn't expect to turn up at all—except for my toes. But that's not important. Is the rest of the plan to be carried out as arranged?'

Juan's lips tightened and he did not answer.

'Listen to me,' I said coldly. 'I haven't time to fool around. Your group has been penetrated and everything you've done or are planning to do is known. I've no way of being sure who can still be trusted and who can't. You may be straight, Juan, or you may also be a police spy. And that goes for everyone else, too. It doesn't matter. I'm going to tell you something and you'll just have to act on it according to what you are.'

While I said all this, I had been easing the revolver out of my belt. 'Now,' flipping the safety catch with my thumb, 'when is the raid on the armoury to take place?'

Juan glanced down at the gun and up at me again with a faint smile. 'Do you think I'd tell you anything because you threatened me?'

'No, I don't. I'm not threatening you, Juan. I'm protecting myself in case you're working with the man I know to be a Central Intelligence Agent.'

'How dare you suggest such a thing!'

'I certainly wouldn't have believed it,' I said: 'but then I'd never had believed it of this man who *is* with the C.I.A. either.'

He gazed at me through narrowed eyes and then he observed: 'You're different.'

'I'm angry,' I explained—'clear through. So God-damned angry I could . . .'

'Yes,' he nodded, 'I can see that.'

'Just shows,' in a lighter tone, 'you can arouse even a literary hack if you kick him around enough.'

'The exact time of the attack hasn't been fixed yet. Everything's ready. We're waiting for El Huero to give us the word to go ahead.'

'I see.' And then, watching Juan's face very closely: 'El Huero's the man.'

'The U.S. agent?'

'Yes.'

'You're mad, of course.'

I shrugged.

'Or else,' he added, 'you're some kind of agent yourself.'

I shrugged again. 'I don't care whether you believe me or not. I didn't expect you to. But if you *are* a patriot, Juan, and if you care anything at all about your comrades, you'll have to check up on what I've said. If there's any chance at all that the raid on the armoury at Melina is a trap, you'll have to warn the others of such a possibility.'

'Have you any proof of what you've said?'

'No. He took me out of jail yesterday to have me killed; but you've only my word for it. Once I'd found out about him, it explained several other things—like Watson's death. But you may have no reasons to doubt him.'

Juan frowned, obviously thinking over what I had told him. 'What are you going to do about it?' he finally asked me.

'I'm not going to tell you. I'm not going to tell anyone, Juan. I'll just have to play it out my own way.'

'Isn't that dangerously individualistic? Suppose something happens to you?'

'Telling you is the only insurance I can think of. You're right, of course. It is individualistic. But it's not false heroics on my part. Frankly, I'd give anything in the world to be able to trust someone else and at least share this awful responsibility. But I blundered into this thing on my own and I'll have to get out of it on my own too.' I laughed bitterly. 'Don't think I fail to appreciate the irony of this responsibility falling on someone so damned inadequate.'

'Perhaps not,' he said. 'As I remarked before—you're different somehow.'

'No,' shaking my head, 'I don't think that. But perhaps when a cause is important enough, it can inspire even the most hopeless with some courage and ingenuity. For everyone's sake I certainly hope so.'

He looked around as Ana came in with a plate of food and some clothes over her arm.

She saw the gun in my hand; but she did not refer to it. She put the plate down on the top of a box and laid the clothes over the railing of one of the stalls. 'These are some things of Juan's. They'll be a bit tight I'm afraid.'

157

Juan was still frowning. He regarded his sister with his lips pursed and then, evidently making up his mind, he said to her: 'Kyle thinks that El Huero is working for the C.I.A.'

'I mentioned that possibility some time ago,' she said with quiet satisfaction.

'So you did!' I recalled. 'Did you have any reason for thinking so?'

'Only an impression I formed after meeting him. He seemed too consciously the great working-class hero shrugging aside the admiration he invited you to feel for him. I disliked him at once and I never can trust anyone I dislike.'

Juan turned to me. 'I'd like to leave now.'

'But what do you think about it?'

He shrugged and smiled enigmatically.

'What are you going to do then?' I asked.

'I'm not going to tell you,' using precisely the words I had used myself. 'I too will have to play it out my own way.'

I stuck the revolver back in my belt. 'Go ahead,' I told him.

'Be careful, Juan,' Ana begged him.

He glanced at her without speaking and went out through the door.

I walked over to the box and hastily finished off the food she had brought. 'I forgot to ask Juan about Manuel Ortiz. Have you heard anything?'

'Only that he's with them in their camp back in the mountains.'

'He's in great danger there. El Huero wouldn't hesitate to kill him.'

'Oh no!' she exclaimed with her hand to her mouth. 'Not after all he's suffered already!'

'I'm afraid so, Ana—unless something can be done quickly.'

I inspected the clothes she had provided. There was a clean shirt which I put on when I had stripped off my own. The jacket was a dress one with fine embroidery ornamenting the lapels. It was a bit tight across the shoulders but I rather fancied myself in it all the same. When I had adjusted the cord of the sombrero under my chin, I turned to face her.

'How do I look now?'

'Still like an American tourist,' she smiled.

'I must go,' I said.

'Kyle . . .'

'Yes?'

'It's not your country.'

'I don't feel that way about it. *Your* country, *Ortiz'* country is as much my country as any other. More so, probably. One's country is that of the people one loves.'

'That's as close to a declaration as I've ever heard you come.'

'Well, I haven't time to go into that now. The main thing is that if bastards like El Huero can swagger around here as though this country belonged to *them,* then it's about time some of the rest of us gringoes started cancelling them out.' I did not try to pursue this idea further. The feeling of desperate urgency which had driven me all the way from the capital was riding me again.

As I walked past her toward the open doors, she caught my arm and held me long enough to kiss me on the cheek. I took off the sombrero and made a sweeping bow, and then hurried away from the stable, leaping the fence at the back and running down the slope through the orange trees.

I did not know if what I was doing could be called working out a plan. I had not changed my mind about wanting to take care of El Huero myself; but thinking it over in daylight had made me realise that it would be extremely irresponsible of me not to make some provision for what was to happen if I failed. All I could do was to spread my knowledge of El Huero's real identity as widely as possible and hope that someone else would take over anything I left unfinished.

Walking through town did not seem to present any major risk of recognition; but even so I tipped my sombrero forward to conceal my face and made my way as inconspicuously as possible around the mercado central and into the maze of unpaved streets beyond. As I approached Pérez' house, there was need for great caution. I walked between two adobe huts and followed the littered alley which twisted along behind the house.

Once I glanced toward the high peaks to the east and thought with an instant regret how safe one would be in those jagged fastnesses. If I ever got out of this, I could look forward to a whole lifetime in which I would never take the slightest chance again. I could imagine myself waiting at a busy street corner and not daring to step off the curb till there was not a single car anywhere in sight! Oh it was going to be very nice indeed just taking excellent care of myself—if I ever got out of this.

I crossed the back yard and rapped on the screen door. In a few moments Rosa appeared and was immediately convulsed with laughter—probably at my garb.

So infectious was it that in spite of my general state of anxiety I could not help getting involved to the extent of a sheepish grin.

Pérez was not there. He was off in his battered car discharging the sort of errand which earned him his daily bread; but Rosa thought he would be back soon and, meanwhile, I was urged to make myself comfortable in that room where I had been held prisoner.

Poor Watson! If only he could have trusted me with his suspicions of El Huero. But that was the difference between people involved in a struggle to liberate their own country and those of us who were interlopers from outside. They developed bonds of trust and a reliable leadership in the course of the fight. We could trust no one, not even ourselves—because our participation was based on individual, not to say arbitrary, choice rather than on a natural response to conditions shared with others. We might have the sort of motives for becoming involved which would be interesting to a novelist; but I would not *trust* us any farther than I could throw a bull by the tail. Indeed, my experiences with the *Review* had taught me not to trust novelists much either.

When Pérez came in about an hour later, I had convinced myself that it was part of my responsibility to make him distrust people like me as we deserved.

'Ah, Señor Kyle,' he greeted me with a warm handshake, his other palm on my shoulder. 'I told them you would succeed. You're a lucky man—like when you got away from the cut-throats in Costaplana. And luck is important.'

'Yes, well my definition of a lucky man is one who doesn't have to go around escaping by the skin of his teeth all the damned time.'

He laughed. 'It was worth running some risks to help set Manuel Ortiz free. You should have been there when he joined us at our camp! We sang songs and recited poetry all night long.'

'How is he, Pérez?'

'Oh he's fine. He insists on coming along when we make our little trip to Melina. He wants people to know that he's marching with us as we set out on the road to freedom.'

'When do you think the attack will take place?'

'Mañana perhaps.' Pérez shrugged. 'El Huero will say.'

'Not Ribera?'

'Ribera makes the plans; but El Huero carries them out.'

'Was El Huero pleased when Ortiz joined you in the mountains?'

'But of course! He made a most wonderful speech. It brought tears to the eyes.'

'He would!' I said sarcastically. 'What if I told you that he was working with our enemies, that he's an American spy?'

'El Huero!'

'El Huero.'

Pérez laughed. 'You're always making jokes, eh, señor? Like coming to my house dressed as a Castillian grandee!'

'Well, I'm as much a Castillian grandee as El Huero's a friend of the people,' I muttered.

'You *are* making a joke, aren't you?' Pérez asked with a slight frown.

'It's a joke, all right—the sort the American government's good at; the sort of joke that people in all the poor countries of the world find simply killing.'

'What are you trying to say, señor?'

'That El Huero's a traitor; but I don't expect you to take my word for it. All I can do, Pérez, is to say what I know and hope that someone will take me seriously enough to try to find out for himself if there's any truth in it.'

'How would *I* find out?' he asked with a deepening frown. 'I am only Pérez who runs errands for those who say they can win back our own country for us. I can only give the revolutionary struggle what little I have, señor.'

I shook my head. 'You *are* the revolution, Pérez.'

He thought about it for a moment and laughed. 'God help us then!'

'God hasn't done much for this country so far. God's been on the side of her enemies—even though he pretended to be with the people.'

'You make God sound like El Huero—if you're right about *him*.'

'They have points in common,' I agreed sardonically.

Pérez scratched his head. 'What are we going to do about it? We could ask El Huero if he's a traitor.'

'I don't somehow think he'd admit it if he was. Do you?'

'Well, señor, you can tell a lot from the way a man denies something. We could ask him tonight.'

'Tonight?'

'There's a meeting at the hut where we took you before —so that the details of the attack can be communicated to those who work underground here in the town. I know about this because I delivered the messages to the ones who are coming—while I was doing my morning rounds.'

'And El Huero will be there?'

'Oh yes. It was El Huero who arranged for me to pass the word along.'

'Are you to be there yourself?'

'No. The meeting's only for section leaders. But I've often gone to places where I wasn't invited. And some-times it leads to *getting* invitations which weren't expected —like the six months' visit I paid to the governor of the jail in Chicoltepec, before Rosa and I moved here where our social life wouldn't take up so much time.'

'I see,' I said thoughtfully.

'At the meeting, señor, you could tell others what you've told me about El Huero. Then he could put his side of the story; and we could all talk it over. Very demo-cratic you see.'

163

'The trouble is that the people who work for the U.S. government only believe in democracy when they know people are going to vote the way they're told to. Otherwise they start shooting.'

'That is true I think; but other people have guns too.'

I gazed steadily at him for a moment or so. 'Do you believe me, Pérez?'

'I don't know. I don't think so, señor. But I like you and so I'm willing to listen.'

'And you trust me enough to take me to the meeting place? I'm very touched.'

'Don't be too touched, señor. If you were working with our enemies, you would only want to know about the meeting; you would not want to go there yourself. Besides, you would not want to do anything bad to Pérez. Pérez is too unimportant.'

'But how could I want to do anything bad to you, anyway? You are my friend.'

'El Huero says he's my friend.'

'You're pretty shrewd, aren't you?'

'Ah, señor, we have to be cunning to survive. And then we have to learn not to let them find out how cunning we are.'

'Of course! No wonder that in the long run you're unbeatable. Me, Pérez, I want to be on the winning side.'

'That I can believe, señor,' he said with a smile.

'It's agreed then that we'll go out there together this evening?'

'That's right. I have some things to do; but you can wait here. Rosa will look after you.'

'Thanks, but I'd prefer to hide up somewhere during the rest of the day. You know that bridge which crosses the stream three or four miles outside of town. About five o'clock I'll be somewhere nearby concealed in the brush. If you stop the car on the other side of the bridge and if no one else is with you, I'll come out and get in.'

'You're pretty shrewd yourself, Señor Kyle.'

'I'm learning, Pérez. As you say, nothing sharpens our wits and our practices, too, like trying to stay alive.'

He put his hand on my shoulder again. 'And we're still friends, eh?'

'Yes of course—friends who have to be a little careful. Someday, perhaps, friends who can trust each other completely.'

'I hope so, señor. Otherwise I would be sorry I liked you. You see, if by not trusting you I came to hate you I would have to avoid you all the time, and I *like* you.'

'I couldn't have put it more neatly myself.'

'And now let us have some coffee and a cigarette. Rosa! Perhaps you should have something to eat, señor, since you may not get another chance. Rosa!! And also you can have some fruit to take away in your pocket. Rosa!!!'

'It'll spoil the line of my jacket, won't it?

'Like the gun stuck in your belt, eh?'

'You weren't supposed to see that, Pérez.'

'I *pretended* not to see it, didn't I?'

'That's true.'

'Pretending can sometimes be a part of friendship too, señor.'

'That's very true.'

'An Ordinary Kitchen Knife'

I had probably done more walking in the last few weeks than in the rest of my life together, I reflected as I picked out a well-concealed spot looking down on the bridge. If I became healthy and sun-tanned as a result of all this, it was not going to do my image as a literato much good.

I sat down with my forearms resting on my knees and my chin on my forearms and tried to think what I would do if I were El Huero. I would have decided by now, since Rómulo and José had not reported back, that something may have gone wrong with my plan to get rid of that tiresome pen-pusher, Brandeis. I might doubt that, even if he were still around, he would have the guts to do anything about the knowledge he had acquired; but with so much at stake I would not let it go at that. No, I would explain to the others that Brandeis had been seen talking to the authorities in the capital, that an attempt had been made to neutralise this threat to their plans, but that if the traitor did turn up he was to be shot on sight.

Then I tried to think whether I would believe what El Huero said if I were one of the others. I had to admit that I probably would.

Therefore, I concluded, it was extremely unlikely that this thing would take the form of a meeting of the college debating society as Pérez had suggested. If I was to be shot on sight, I would rather not appear at all. Much as it might go against my more gentlemanly instincts, the smartest and safest thing to do was to shoot El Huero in the back. Well, hadn't he just that moment been doubting if I had any guts! Served him right then if I skulked about and fired at him from the shadows like the coward I was.

I looked at my watch. Where was Pérez? Considering the shape that car of his was in, it was only at best an even chance that he would arrive at the bridge at all. I began to wonder whether I was more afraid that he would or would not make our rendezvous. If something prevented me from getting up to the hut and doing what I had to do, I would not be able to live with myself. If nothing stopped me, I most likely would not be around any more for me or anyone else to live with. I tried to convince myself that since I looked like losing out either way, I could afford to be indifferent about the alternatives; but the jumpy beat of my heart and the heavy feeling in the pit of my stomach assured me that I had not succeeded. Where in the hell was Pérez?

And then, a bit after five, I heard a car coming from town. It crossed the bridge and stopped. Pérez got out and opened all the doors to show that no one was hiding inside. He stood in the road and turning to various points of the compass struck his breast and held up one finger.

Smiling at this pantomime I came out of my cover and trotted down the slope.

We got inside and, after five or six attempts while I held my breath, Pérez coaxed the engine into spluttering life. I did not feel like talking and we hardly exchanged a word as we chugged up toward the pass, the car beginning to steam like a locomotive as it heated up on the long up-hill pull.

We rolled down into the eerie desolation of the valley beyond, already half in shadow as the sun declined behind the western wall.

When we reached the spot where we had left the car before, I asked Pérez: 'Aren't you going to try to conceal the car? You could drive it behind those boulders.'

'Not necessary. It's better if I am quite open in what I am doing, señor. I intend to be present at the meeting. I was not asked to come but I was not told to stay away. No one will object to my being there, I think.'

'Perhaps you're right.'

'You're coming too, aren't you?—to raise the question of El Huero's loyalty.'

'Well, I hadn't thought of sitting down around the table with them.'

'What are you going to do, then?'

'I'm not going to tell you, Pérez—partly because I don't know myself. Are *you* going to do anything about El Huero?'

'I shall make some enquiries. I shall ask some questions.'

'Good.' I held out my hand. 'We part company here— at least for the time being.'

'Be careful,' he warned.

'I'll take as good care of myself as possible.'

'I did not mean only that, señor. If you start shooting with that gun you've acquired, try to miss me, will you?'

'Missing things with this gun is something I'm pretty expert at,' I assured him. 'In fact, shooting first and asking questions later makes sense when it's *my* finger on the trigger.'

'Good luck, Señor Kyle.'

'One more thing,' I turned back to enquire. 'Will there be a guard at the hut as early as this?'

'There's always a guard there.'

'That's what I thought. Well, adios, Pérez.'

'Hasta la vista,' he corrected optimistically.

I waited till he had begun ascending the path before addressing myself to the arduous task of finding another way up the steep slope. It was my intention to get to the top of the ridge and then see if I could approach the hut by climbing down the abrupt cliff behind it.

I walked back along the dusty track and circled a spur of rock slanting down onto the desert floor. Beyond it a precipitous ravine gouged out of the sandstone bluff seemed to provide hand and foot holds a considerable way upward. I stripped off the ornate jacket and left it at the foot of the cliff.

The going was not bad for the first hundred feet or so and then I ran into trouble. The ravine became for a few yards an almost vertical chimney and then petered out altogether. To make matters worse, the red sandstone was soft and crumbly and what looked like solid projections would go to pieces when weight was put on them. I found myself, legs straddled too wide for comfort, fingers desperately digging into a small lateral crevice, unable to go higher and extremely doubtful about even returning the way I had come. As my knees began to tremble with strain and sweat poured down my face and made my hands slippery I realised that I could not stay where I was either.

Neck muscles aching with the effort to look upward without throwing my body too far back to maintain my balance, I searched frantically for some means of extricating myself. Above and to my right, laminations in the sandstone seemed to offer the chance of a kind of ladder which might get me over the outward bulge of the bluff; but reaching it would involve moving my left foot from its support while thrusting up as far as I could on my right foot and at the same time grabbing with the tips of my fingers for that first crack in the stone. But I doubted if my right leg, now shaking badly, could give me the full upward push I needed. And if my fingers failed to grip the tiny ledge, I would never be able to recover the position I was precariously maintaining.

Still, my strength was ebbing away as I clung there. I would fall anyway if I did not do something quickly. I closed my eyes a moment and tried to rally all the force and control I had left. Then, with a sudden movement before my resolution could desert me, I swung into that difficult contorted try for the ledge. I missed with one hand and went sick and cold in the instant that I felt myself going. But in the next moment I had managed somehow to get both hands firmly wedged and I was all right. I sighed so deeply with relief that I blew some of the particles of red rock dust in my face and laughed at this trifling mishap.

There were no other hazards to compare with that terrible scramble on the vertical face. I climbed to the top of the ridge and stretched out on the warm stone utterly exhausted. When there were those so eager to kill me, I thought, it was very selfish to gamble with my life that way.

The sun had disappeared by the time I got to my feet and started walking along the rocky crest to a point just above the hut. The whole west was a magnificent burnished bronze shot through with streaks of crimson. 'Not now!' I said rather impatiently. 'Some other evening perhaps—preferably with Ana in the offing.'

When I considered that I had gone far enough along the top, I looked over the edge and saw the roof of the hut far below and slightly to the right. I did not want to make my descent directly in line with the hut for fear of dislodging stones which might be heard by anyone inside.

I carefully worked out a possible route down the slope which, though steep, was not so precipitous as my way up had been. I studied every detail of the course I intended to follow while waiting for it to get darker.

At last I began, slowly and very cautiously, to climb down. As long as I stuck to the zigzag path I had worked out and watched where I placed each foot, I ought to be able to come down behind the hut undetected. This side of the slope was already washed in thick shadow.

I slid around a rock rib and was only about twenty yards above the hut. I remained there for some time, hidden in a natural recess, while I watched for any sign of movement on the ledge or on the pathway leading up to it. Anyone around must be inside the hut.

The hut was set into the cliff side so that the roof jutted out from the rocks buttressing the rear wall. I crept down to this juncture and found that there was a gap of four or five inches between the edge of the roof and the top of the back wall which it overhung—no doubt to afford more ventilation than the two small windows in front provided. By lying down in the hollow where the rocks met this back wall about two feet from the top, I could peer through this gap and see inside the hut.

A lamp had already been lit and stood on the table at which El Huero had sat during our first interview. There were three men within—Pérez and two others, both armed, whom I had never seen before. They sat on their heels with their backs against the wall, drawing at brown paper cigarettes and occasionally exchanging a few words which I could not catch. One of them got up and adjusted the wick of the lamp so that it would not smoke and then squatted down again.

I watched them for a while and then began to get uneasy at the thought that there might be a search of the immediate vicinity before the meeting began. I got up and withdrew to the recess in the rocks from which I had made my first survey. If there *was* any move toward having a good look around the hut, I would at least have some chance of retreating up the slope.

In the late dusk a small party came up the path and entered the hut. Later still, when night had fallen, I saw torches down below; and a larger group, probably from the base camp farther back in the mountains, climbed to the ledge and went inside.

I continued to wait for another fifteen or twenty minutes. There was no moon yet, but the stars were so bright in a perfectly clear sky that darkness did not seem complete. The open strip just under the roof glowed orangely from the lamp inside; and after making myself hold on while I counted out another ten minutes I moved cautiously down to it, taking infinite care with every step.

I lowered myself into the gully behind the back wall and looked through the gap.

With a shock of hatred and fear I saw El Huero's broad back as he bent over the table on which a map was spread. I saw Juan Gabaldon on the other side of the room from Pérez, and a dozen others I did not know.

Jones's hair looked white in the lamplight as he talked in low tones and from time to time stabbed at the map with a blunt forefinger. He paused and looked around the room and then went on again, calm and unhurried and so apparently sure of himself that I could almost have doubted what I knew of him. Indeed, for an instant I had the terrible feeling that I must be mistaken, and what had happened in the capital might be susceptible of some explanation which would show that he still deserved the unquestioning attention he was receiving. So strong was this disturbing sensation it almost seemed that *I*, skulking about in the shadows, was the enemy bent on disrupting the plan they were discussing, *I* the traitor who was trying to destroy them.

El Huero looked up from the map again. Juan was

speaking, voice raised so that his words came to me quite distinctly.

'Are you sure,' he asked, 'that it's safe to go through with the attack?'

'As safe as such things can ever be.'

'But you told us,' Juan went on, 'that Brandeis had been seen at the American Embassy. Didn't *he* know about the attack on the armoury?'

'Not unless you told him.' El Huero straightened and pointing his finger at Juan demanded: '*Did* you tell him? He was thick enough with your sister.'

'Watson told him and you know it.' Juan looked around, seeking corroboration from Pérez.

But El Huero took advantage of the confusion this exchange had caused and shouted: 'Grab that man. He may have betrayed us. We'll get the truth out of him one way or another.'

Pérez started to get up but the man next to him took hold of his arm. Juan too was tightly gripped by the men on each side of him and there was a general cry for 'the truth!' echoing El Huero's insinuation.

I had eased the revolver out of my belt and I poked it through the gap sighting down at El Huero's back. I waited to see if there was any hope of a reasonable investigation of the charges that had been made. As the confusion grew and was obviously being used by El Huero to get rid of the only two men there who knew he was lying, I took up the slack in the trigger.

This had to be good. With the muzzle resting on the wood for steadiness and with the sights carefully lined on a point between El Huero's shoulder blades I did not see how I could possibly miss. I squeezed the trigger slowly and there was a loud report which sounded thunderous in the confined space of the room.

El Huero was driven forward by the impact of the

bullet; but he did not fall. I could see the spreading stain on his right shoulder. I fired again, quickly, missing him altogether. And by then El Huero was moving too fast for me to shoot again without the risk of hitting someone else.

He whirled and I had one brief glimpse of that dark, freckled face showing no sign of panic as he swept up the lamp and hurled it against the wall. It smashed and spread flaming kerosene all around, sending several men running toward the door beating at their burning clothes.

Others had also rushed for the door causing a momentary jam in the entrance. But a man on the opposite side of the room jerked his pistol from its holster and fired twice in my direction. A splinter of wood laid open my cheek as I rolled away and scrambled back among the rocks.

Below me there was complete confusion now. Dark figures rushed about on the ledge and there was a lot of shouting and cursing. Several more shots were fired and someone yelled: 'Cut that out!' The gap between roof and wall glowed redder as the fire burned up inside the hut. Smoke began to leak out into the night in grey wisps which turned to rose as the flames licked around the dry wood.

What was I supposed to do? I wondered frantically. I was like a little boy who has stirred up a wasps' nest without thinking what he is going to do when the damned things furiously swarm out.

Where was El Huero? I had been watching the front part of the hut since I had moved back to my vantage point among the rocks; but I had no way of knowing whether he had come outside yet. Others might dash around aimlessly in the dark; but not El Huero. I could still see that determined face, grimly mocking in its self assurance, as he had instantaneously done exactly the right thing to escape from a badly-sprung trap. That I had even dared to try to kill a man like him seemed to me the most reckless act of wanton provocation. El Huero would not be dashing about aimlessly. He would be hunting down with a ruthless efficiency those who had attacked him. I knew I ought to make up my mind at once to try to finish the job I had bungled or to get out of there as fast as I could; but I simply cowered there among the rocks in a kind of numbed trance at the thought of the vindictive force I had loosed into the night.

Snake tongues of fire darted out from under the roof and orange light played flickeringly about the rocky recess where I was hiding. Soon the burning hut would illuminate the whole cliff side like a giant flaring torch; and still I did nothing, as motionless as a beady-eyed rabbit watching a rattler. I *wanted* to scamper up the slope to the top of the ridge; but I was held there by the knowledge that Juan and, perhaps, Pérez were in just as great danger. And yet I could not make myself do anything about it.

As the fire swept along the top of the hut I realised that I no longer enjoyed any concealment at all. I was perched up there in the full blaze of the flames, like a statue in a niche, for anyone down below to take pot shots at. Besides, it was getting too hot there.

I climbed around a broken rib of stone and began working my way along the steep face away from the hut. When I looked back, the heat of the fire seemed to have turned the frame structure transparent, only the heavier beams standing out darkly against the incandescent core.

Balancing myself on a narrow ledge I tried to remember how many shots I had fired. Two or three. Anyway, I had better reload the revolver.

My hands were trembling as I broke the gun and rather clumsily began replacing the used cartridges. I was standing there like that when I heard a low laugh of thoroughly satisfied triumph.

I looked up and there was El Huero grinning down at me from behind a small spire of rock about ten yards higher up the cliff.

Frantically I tried to snap the revolver back into readiness and—it slipped out of my hands to clatter on the rocks at my feet.

Again, that same smug laugh. The fire behind me lit that smiling face and dark freckles stood out individually in the bright glow. Freckles, boyhood, healthy innocence and that gloating vicious stare flashed across my mind in an instant incongruity as I stood there paralysed.

One powerful shoulder jutted out from the stone. An arm came into sight and then the broad freckled fist with the gun like a metallic forefinger rising to point at me in fatal distinction.

I jerked my eyes away from the gun to look up at his face. There was a slow, almost pitying shake of his head for anyone who had been so stupid as to try to buck him at his own game. The reflection of the flames played over the tightening muscles at the corners of his square jaws, over the rocks turned blood red in that wavering light, and over something else in the darkness beyond.

Someone moved in the darkness beyond. I stared hard as a man moved out of the deep shadows and braced himself on a narrow shelf.

Jones watched my eyes fixed behind him and once more there was that slight contemptuous shake of his head, dismissing with a faint smile that oldest trick in the book of the utterly desperate.

All this while the gun came up level with my chest and my knees sagged and only the pressure of my weight kept the hand on the stone from shaking violently.

'El Huero!'

I could see who it was then in the shifting light—my friend of the night before, Rómulo.

A quick frown instantly knotted Jones's sandy brows as the voice repeated with the same insistence: 'El Huero!'

Then, showing that remarkable co-ordination of mind and muscle which had already saved him once that night, El Huero whirled and fired in one swift movement.

The two guns made a single explosion tailing off in the whine of Rómulo's bullet slanting off the rocks. El Huero's second shot caught him full in the chest, slamming him back against the stone face.

But I was already retreating in a wild flailing crab-like scramble slanting toward the crest. Hands and knees were torn and bruised as I threw every bit of energy I had into that mad diagonal dash up the steep slope. Small stones slid out from under me and went cascading down below. Only that frantic impetus in which fingers, elbows, knees and feet were all violently employed in propelling myself up and away carried me over precarious places where the law of gravity had a legitimate claim to my body.

I knew El Huero could not be far behind me. I knew he had killed Rómulo. In fact, I could no longer imagine any situation in which he would not come off victorious. My own death was fixed from the moment I realised who he really was, and the greatest efforts I could make would amount to no more than a dubious postponement.

Somewhere off to my left I could hear someone calling. It took me a few moments in my concentration on using every knob of rock and tuft of grass to realise that it was my name which was being shouted. Juan was telling me to angle my flight in his direction.

But he must not have been aware of the perpendicular cleft which cut off that possibility. Several shots were fired below me and I did not hear Juan's voice any more.

I was getting clumsier with near exhaustion and coming closer to falling. And worse, I did not even care very much. I had just about reached the point where staying alive was too costly an effort. In another minute or so the balance would have shifted far enough that I would give up. Giving up really began to appeal to me as a relatively pleasant alternative.

I pushed away from the cliff to see how far it still was to the top and a bullet chipped the stone beside my hand. There were only a few feet more to go. I would get to the top and then I would give up. Getting to the top would not make all that difference. El Huero would reach it a few seconds later. But I would force myself to make that one last effort and then to hell with it!

Gasping for breath, shaking so violently I seemed to have lost all articulation, drenched with sweat which poured down me and turned clammy cold in the night air I finally pulled myself up over the lip of the ridge and sprawled on the flat stone surface.

I rolled over on my back, arms flung wide, and stared up into the black star-studded sky. I shook my head slowly from side to side, as much as to say: 'That's that. I can't do more.'

As my head sagged to the right I caught a glimpse out of the corner of my eye of a man kneeling on one knee. He came up to a crouch as I watched, turned his face toward me showing a wide grin and moved forward to the edge.

It was Pérez.

I came up on one elbow and called: 'Look out! He's right behind me.'

Pérez made a motion with one hand for me to keep quiet. His other hand lightly held what looked like an ordinary kitchen knife.

I twisted about on the stone so that I could peer over

the rim. The hut was burning as fiercely as the last time I had seen it. So crowded had been the moments since, that I must have expected it to have diminished by then to glowing embers. Silhouetted against the glow of the flames was El Huero.

He came up the slope, carefully picking footholds and only requiring an occasional push with the fingers of his left hand to maintain his progress. Not much like my own furious ascent! The hand holding the revolver moved about expertly to help him keep his balance.

His head bent backwards so that he could look up to the top, the thick muscles of his neck cording in the effort. He saw Pérez and pushed away from the cliff to bring up the gun. He was standing poised like that when I was aware of Pérez' rapid movement and the black haft of the knife suddenly appeared in the middle of El Huero's wide chest.

His eyes were full of momentary disbelief. I could hardly believe it myself. I watched with growing conviction as El Huero, very slowly it seemed, leaned backward. Very slowly, standing quite straight, he leaned farther and farther away from the rocky face. He appeared enormous to me leaning backward into the air which was alive with sparks of fire from the blazing hut.

His head and shoulders continued to describe that slow arc for an appreciable moment and then his body bent and he went tumbling down the slope in a shower of pebbles and dust to lie broken and awkward on the rocks just above the leaping flames.

Pérez laughed. 'You set that up very well, Señor Kyle.'

'Sure,' I said sarcastically. 'I planned the whole thing—even down to pretending to be scared to death in order to lure him on. I'm quite a guy.'

Juan came along the ridge and joined us.

'Thank Christ,' I breathed. 'I thought he had shot you, too.'

'No; but he drove me back into the rocks for cover. When Pérez and I saw where he had gone, we split up to try to reach you from two directions. Then you walked straight into his arms and we thought you were done for.'

'I would've been, if it hadn't been for Rómulo suddenly turning up.'

'What happened to him?'

'Killed I'm afraid.'

'He was a strange one, that Rómulo.'

'He saved my life twice—for what it's worth . . . You know there's a lot to be said for a sedentary existence. Running a small literary review now, in a quiet university town . . .'

12

'A Red Carpet of Ponchos'

THERE was nothing much left of the hut and the fire was beginning to die down. An occasional crack of collapsing brands still sent fountains of sparks into the air and in the red glow of fanned embers the twisted figure of El Huero was plainly visible on the rocks.

'We had better go,' Juan said. 'Perhaps we can find some of the others below and explain what's happened.'

I looked down the slope and then held out my lacerated hands. 'I don't think I can clamber about on this damned cliff much more.'

'You've got a bad cut on your cheek too,' Juan said.

I noticed for the first time that blood from the gash opened up by a flying splinter had dripped down and darkened my shirt. 'I left that splendid jacket of yours somewhere at the bottom.'

Juan shrugged. 'No matter.'

'I'll tell you what we can do,' Pérez suggested. 'You two can walk along the ridge. After a while it slants down in easy steps. I'll get the car and pick you up where the road begins to climb up to the pass.'

'Good,' Juan agreed. 'See if you can find any of the others.'

'I want my knife also,' Pérez grinned. 'That has always been a lucky knife for me.'

'And for me,' I muttered fervently.

I took a last look at the smouldering ruin of the hut

and that dark broken body; and I followed Juan along the crest.

We did not talk much. I was too tired and, anyway, I knew I could not really express the peculiar satisfaction I felt at El Huero's death. It was like the expunging of some monstrous perversion that was a libel on all us gringoes. I had not killed him, it was true; but I realised that a more perfect piece of justice had been achieved through the agency of Pérez. Somehow it represented for me this whole struggle, not only here but all over the world, in which the damned of the earth were standing up, standing up and fighting back. El Huero had seemed invincible to me; but Pérez had got rid of him—with a kitchen knife.

The car was waiting for us when we reached the road. Pérez contrived to look exceedingly little like a symbol of national liberation as he laughed and chatted on the drive back to town—but that itself, I decided, was most symbolic of all.

He dropped us off at the house where Juan stayed when he was in town.

I was so utterly exhausted that I could hardly keep my eyes open while a kindly woman attended to my cuts and abrasions.

I tumbled gratefully onto a canvas cot provided for me and did not wake up till late the next morning. Juan had already left.

I was given breakfast and coffee and, while I smoked a cigarette, I realised that I was sufficiently recovered from the events of the previous night to begin worrying about what I was going to do next. My affairs in the States must be in a hell of a mess. The *Review*, which had never been noted for regularity of publication, looked like never appearing again unless I could get down to work.

I was kicking around an idea concerning the fate of

the thriller as a literary genre if the frustration of intellectuals which had given rise to it got swallowed up in
violent action when Juan returned.

'Come,' he urged. 'There's something we have to do.'

He handed me a clean shirt to put on.

'I hope you've got an extensive wardrobe,' I told him.
'We seem to be running through your clothes at a remarkable rate. My own are scattered about in hotels all
over the country.'

I dressed and went outside with him.

'Oh no!' I exclaimed when I saw the car parked in
front of the house with the man at the wheel who had
driven Watson and me to Costaplana.

'What's the matter?' Juan asked.

'It's this promise I made. I vowed that if I got out
alive last night I wouldn't risk my neck for at least
twenty-four hours. I hate breaking promises—particularly to myself.'

Miguel seemed delighted to see me again and insisted
that on a pleasure trip like this one he was prepared to
take his time.

I did not believe him for a moment; but I allowed myself to be persuaded to get inside.

Sure enough, my back had hardly touched the seat
when we were away with a screech of tires.

'It sounds worse than it is, señor,' Miguel turned
around to explain. 'In hot countries the tires are soft and
always make that noise.'

I implored him to watch the road and spare me his
lectures on popular science. 'I'm an arts man myself,' I
pointed out firmly.

Miguel took a corner on two wheels and headed for the
centre of town.

'Where are we going?' I asked Juan.

'To the camp in the mountains. But first we have to pick up someone.'

'Anybody I know?'

'Well yes,' he said with a certain embarrassment. 'Ana.'

'Ana!'

'I was surprised too. You see, she's been working with Ribera all along—reporting to him on things going on in town, deciding who among the better-off people could be trusted to the extent of being asked to provide funds, and all that.'

'Well I'm damned!'

'It *is* a little disconcerting,' Juan agreed. 'When I think of the times I've argued that her phoney liberalism wasn't enough in the present situation.'

I was rather miserably aware that this fact explained an interest in me which I had ascribed to something else altogether. What a fool I must have looked, going all noble and half-heartedly trying to talk her out of being attracted to me when she had merely been doing a job of work. And her suspicions of El Huero of course, which I had laughed off as a particularly inept piece of feminine intuition! For all I knew, she had simply been using me to expose him. I decided that the only dignified course I could take when we met was to sulk.

The car pulled up not far from the cathedral. Juan moved up front with Miguel and Ana got in beside me.

'I'm so glad you're all right, Kyle,' she said and laid her hand on my forearm.

'All right!' I protested. 'Look at my hands. I don't think all the cactus spines have been removed even now. I won't be able to hold a pen between those fingers for weeks; and for a man in my profession that could mean starvation.'

'I'm afraid,' she smiled, 'I was worried about something much worse.'

'Worse than starvation! And besides,' turning to consider that lovely face, 'for someone worried half to death you don't seem to have missed out on your beauty sleep.'

'I knew what had happened last night. One of the men who was in that hut is a very close comrade of mine. He gave me a full account of the whole thing. Furthermore, he was there to look out for you.'

'Well,' not entirely mollified, 'he didn't do a very good job of it.'

'And he apologised humbly for losing sight of you in the confusion when the fire started.'

'You can tell him I accept his apology,' I said magnanimously, though I still felt a little that I might have been used as a tethered goat to lure El Huero out into the open.

I had been staring at her rather closely to try to guess what she really thought of me when she said : 'Have I got a smudge on my face?'

'No, it's just that your beauty helps distract me from Miguel's driving.'

'I don't believe you've ever described me as beautiful before.'

'You're not suggesting that it comes as a surprise to you.'

'I'm not nearly so interested in what I'm like as in what *you* think I'm like.'

I cocked one eyebrow at her. '*Now* what have you got in mind?' I asked suspiciously. 'Perhaps you'd like the president assassinated or some little thing like that.'

'I might have known you'd take the typical male attitude of resenting my being involved in politics.'

'Just your involving *me* in politics.'

'That's merely a pretence, Kyle. You couldn't stay out of something like this if your life depended on it.'

'It very nearly did.'

185

The car sped over the pass and down into that arid
valley enclosed in red sandstone cliffs. I thought I could
see a few wisps of smoke where the hut had been. At
the end of the valley a narrow road cut through the bluffs
and curved up into the hills beyond. Soon we were in the
mountains and I could judge our height from the coolness of the clear morning air.

An hour later, after a zigzag trip among the heights,
often skirting patches of snow, Miguel pulled up and we
got out.

'We go the rest of the way on foot,' Juan told me.

Miguel turned the car around and started back as the
three of us went single file down a steep path.

'The trouble with national liberation struggles,' I complained at the rear of our little party, 'is that they involve
such a hell of a lot of walking. We gringoes aren't used
to so much strenuous activity.'

'That's one of the reasons we'll win in the end,' Juan
said.

'That and your utter ruthlessness,' I commented. 'In
some places guerrilla forces quite deliberately cut off supplies of comic books intended for the American soldiers
committing mayhem there.'

It took us about an hour to reach the camp; and when
we got there it looked as though the camp was about to be
moved somewhere else. Several tents had already been
struck and equipment was collected in a large pile to be
transported.

Juan pointed out a very solidly built man standing in
front of the only tent which had not been touched yet.
'That's Ribera. He wants to meet you.'

Ribera had a typically Indian face with high cheek-
bones and very black eyes, deep set and heavy-lidded,
fanning out at the corners in tiny wrinkles. He smiled as
we approached showing strong white teeth.

'Ah,' he said, holding out his hand, 'the tourist from the north!'

'Maybe,' I agreed reluctantly; 'but I'll bet no one's ever gone to greater lengths to try to avoid it.'

'If all tourists were like you, my friend, the people of this country would lay a red carpet of ponchos all the way to the Rio Grande.'

I was very touched. No official ceremony in which I was decorated for some accidental act of gallantry could have meant as much to me.

'Come inside.' Ribera held back the tent flap. 'Another good friend of yours is here.'

I ducked and entered and saw Manuel Ortiz, a serape around his shoulders to ward off the coolness of that high air. He got up and embraced me and made me sit on the camp stool beside him.

Juan and Ana had also come inside and shortly afterwards we were brought hot drinks.

Ortiz put his hand on my arm. 'I've often told the comrades here how you fooled that pompous official in the prison.'

'Did you know that I was put into your old cell when the police picked me up? I wish I'd brought you that cook book as a souvenir.'

'How did you get out?'

'That was easy. El Huero pretended to be helping me to escape so that he could have me bumped off. Fortunately Rómulo had been won over by you,' smiling at Ribera. 'He killed the other man and I came back to San Pedro.'

'You've had a very adventurous holiday,' Ribera nodded.

Ortiz said with a laugh: 'You must never underestimate us literary men.'

'I didn't do anything but get myself in one scrape after

another,' I said. 'I was just lucky in having friends who always helped me out.'

'Having friends like that is not a question of luck,' Ortiz insisted. 'I think, like me, you must have a *taste* for adventure. The pen may be mightier than the sword; but there are times when the latter is more appropriate.'

'Well,' ruefully, 'I'm a lot more dangerous with a good sharp quill pen, I suspect, than with a revolver.'

'What will you do now?' Ribera asked me with a lift of his brows.

'Go back to the States I suppose,' without much enthusiasm.

'You can't do that I'm afraid. Don't you realise that El Huero will have mentioned you in his reports? You'd be arrested the moment you crossed the border.'

'I suppose I can go back to England then.'

'Do you doubt that England would surrender you to the U.S. if pressed?'

'Not these days,' I had to admit.

'And you can't remain openly in our country either. Even if the government here did not want to hold you themselves they would agree to your extradition.'

'I hadn't thought of that.'

'You see,' with a gesture toward the activity outside the tent, 'we are having to leave here ourselves. We know that reports of everything we have been doing are probably in the hands of the government.'

'What are *you* going to do then?' I asked.

'We're moving north to the jungle around Rosario. It's the country I know best. We shall be quiet for a while and then start up once more with greater support. Ortiz is coming with us. He will help rally people to our side.'

'Well,' I scratched my head, 'I don't know *what* I can

do. I'll have to think about it when I get back to San Pedro.'

Ribera shook his head. 'You can't even go back there I'm afraid. They'll be looking for you now I should think, waiting for you to come back to your hotel.'

'There goes my last pair of pajamas and another tooth-brush!' I complained.

'You don't seem to realise yet what it means to have had a traitor in our midst all these months. These young people here,' nodding toward Juan and Ana, 'they can't go back. They're coming with us when we march north.'

'Are you suggesting that I should come with you?'

'We've talked about it, Ortiz and I and the others. We don't believe any other course would be safe for you. Later perhaps it may be possible for you to leave. We have contacts with those outside who are sympathetic to our cause. Later we could arrange for you to get away by boat.'

'I see. But won't I be a nuisance? Hell, I can't even shoot!'

'We can teach you. But there're other things you can do. People in the States must know why we're fighting. You can tell them. You can explain why our fight is their fight too. You can show them that the enemies of a peaceful prosperous country down here are the enemies of peace in their land as well, that their young men are serving the interests of a wicked minority when they allow themselves to be shipped all over the world in the defence of capitalism.'

'It looks as though the long-haired, egg-head reader-ship of the *Western Review* might be in for some surprises.' On reflection I wondered if the possibility of writing the sort of articles Ribera was referring to might not account for the difficulty I had found in dashing off my usual stuff. I seemed to have lost my capacity for literary fiddling while the world was on fire.

I got up and said : 'I'd like to think about all this.'

'Of course,' Ribera nodded.

I went outside and walked over to one of the fires blazing brightly as various articles which could not be taken on the march were thrown into the flames. Room was made for me and I saw Pérez standing there with the others.

'You're coming with us, Señor Kyle?' he asked with pleasure.

'I don't know. What've you done about Rosa?'

'Oh she's coming.' He made a face. 'I told her about the hardships of the journey; but she just laughed.'

'And the car?'

'I turned it into one of those.' He pointed to the burros which would be used to carry the heavier equipment. 'Tomás will be joining us later with Rosa. She'll be riding on the donkey, I think—though I told Tomás to make her walk. It's only a *little* donkey. It was such an *old* car.'

'It may be a long time before we see another bull fight together, Pérez.'

'There'll be other kinds of excitement—as long as you're around.'

'I know. I'm like an empty place, waiting for something to happen in it.'

Pérez was called away to join a group of men who were folding up one of the tents.

I remained standing by the fire feeling very unsettled by all the preparations for departure. I wanted to go with them; but it would be such a definitive break with my whole past life. True, it had not been much of a life; and yet it was difficult to write it off like that.

'What are you thinking about, Kyle?'

I turned to look at Ana who had come over to stand beside me.

'Oh, lots of things,' I told her.

'You really haven't much choice about going with us, have you?'

'Not much.'

'Are you sorry?'

'Nope. That's the trouble. It's what I want to do so I have to make sure there's no alternative. I always feel that anything I want to do *must* be wrong.'

'You're probably thinking about all those ex-wives you won't see again.'

'That's not the only reason I want to join the march; but it's a pretty cogent one.'

'Of course,' with a quick glance from those lovely eyes, 'you may think that without any wives at all life would be too pleasant and you'd just feel miserably guilty; but perhaps something could be done about that.'

'Look, Ana, if you're using your wiles on me because you think I might be useful you're wasting your time.'

'Oh,' she said rather stiffly.

'Wasting your time,' I went on, 'in the sense that there's no point in plastering a target which has already been demolished. Anyone carrying the weapons you do has to be a bit careful about the problem of overkill.'

'You don't know much about women, do you?'

'I ought to. I studied the subject in a hard school.'

'It wouldn't occur to you that it might work the other way as well, that I might use winning you over to our side as an excuse for throwing myself at you in a most unladylike way.'

'It *might* occur to me, if I could see any reason for your personal interest.'

'You can stop talking like that, Kyle,' she told me quite sternly. 'I used to think you were guilty of false modesty. But it isn't that. You simply don't want to make any move yourself, so that you can avoid responsibility for anything that happens.'

'Well, twice bitten . . .'

'But it forces *me* to make all the running.'

'You'd better slow down, or you'll shoot right past me. Besides we're going to need all our energy for traipsing around this land afoot.'

'You're coming with us, then?'

'It looks that way.'

Impulsively she threw her arms around me and kissed me. Then, leaning away and glancing up at my face, 'I know you're happy, Kyle. You look so woebegone.'

Pérez came back to the fire with an airline bag and a panama hat. 'I almost forgot, Señor Kyle. I slipped into your hotel room and got these. I could not find your suitcase.'

'Olé!' I exclaimed.

I reached inside the bag and found my toothbrush. 'What more could a man want?' I put the hat on my head and, arranging the mountain peaks behind me as a spectacular background, assumed a posture I imagined to be like that of stout Cortez. 'How do I look?'

Pérez eyed me quizzically. 'Like a hobo, señor?'

'Well,' shrinking back to life size, 'that's an advance on any other offers I've had.'